...OIR

Also by Janet Frame

Novels

Stories and Sketches

Poetry

Autobiography

THE RESERVOIR

STORIES AND SKETCHES

JANET FRAME

GEORGE BRAZILLER • NEW YORK

100419 6448

The stories "Prizes" and "The Reservoir" appeared originally in The New Yorker Magazine.

to R. H. C.

CONTENTS

the reservoir

It was said to be four or five miles along the gully, past orchards and farms, paddocks filled with cattle, sheep, wheat, gorse, and the squatters of the land who were the rabbits eating like modern sculpture into the hills, though how could we know anything of modern sculpture, we knew nothing but the Warrior in the main street with his wreaths of poppies on Anzac Day, the gnomes weeping in the Gardens because the seagulls perched on their green caps and showed no respect, and how important it was for birds, animals and people, especially children, to show respect!

And that is why for so long we obeyed the command of the grownups and never walked as far as the forbidden Reservoir, but were content to return "tired but happy" (as we wrote in our school compositions), answering the question, Where did you walk today? with a suspicion of blackmail, "Oh, nearly, nearly to the Reservoir!"

The Reservoir was the end of the world; beyond it, you fell; beyond it were paddocks of thorns, strange cattle, strange farms, legendary people whom we would never know or recognize even if they walked among us on a Friday night downtown when we went to follow the boys and listen to the Salvation Army Band and buy a milk shake in the milk bar and then return home to find that everything was all right and safe, that our mother had not run away and caught the night train to the North Island, that our father had not shot himself with worrying over the bills, but had in fact been downtown himself and had bought the usual Friday night treat, a bag of licorice all-sorts and a bag of chocolate roughs, from Woolworth's.

The Reservoir haunted our lives. We never knew one until we came to this town; we had used pump water. But here, in our new house, the water ran from the taps as soon as we turned them on, and if we were careless and left them on, our father would shout, as if the affair were his personal concern, "Do you want the Reservoir to run dry?"

That frightened us. What should we do if the Reservoir ran dry? Would we die of thirst like Burke and Wills in the desert?

"The Reservoir," our mother said, "gives pure water, water safe to drink without boiling it."

The water was in a different class, then, from the creek which flowed through the gully; yet the creek had its source in the Reservoir. Why had it not received the pampering attention of officialdom which strained weed and earth, cockabullies and trout and eels, from our tap water? Surely the Reservoir was not entirely pure?

"Oh no," they said, when we inquired. We learned that

the water from the Reservoir had been "treated." We supposed this to mean that during the night men in light-blue uniforms with sacks over their shoulders crept beyond the circle of pine trees which enclosed the Reservoir, and emptied the contents of the sacks into the water, to dissolve dead bodies and prevent the decay of teeth.

Then, at times, there would be news in the paper, discussed by my mother with the neighbors over the back fence. Children had been drowned in the Reservoir.

"No child," the neighbor would say, "ought to be allowed near the Reservoir."

"I tell mine to keep strictly away," my mother would reply.

And for so long we obeyed our mother's command, on our favorite walks along the gully simply following the untreated cast-off creek which we loved and which flowed day and night in our heads in all its detail—the wild sweet peas, boiled-lolly pink, and the mint growing along the banks; the exact spot in the water where the latest dead sheep could be found, and the stink of its bloated flesh and floating wool, an allowable earthy stink which we accepted with pleasant revulsion and which did not prompt the "inky-pinky I smell Stinkie" rhyme which referred to offensive human beings only. We knew where the water was shallow and could be paddled in, where forts could be made from the rocks; we knew the frightening deep places where the eels lurked and the weeds were tangled in gruesome shapes; we knew the jumping places, the mossy stones with their dangers, limitations, and advantages; the sparkling places where the sun trickled beside the water, upon the stones; the bogs made by roaming cattle, trapping some of them to death; their gaunt telltale bones; the little valleys with their new growth of lush grass where the creek had "changed its course," and no longer flowed.

"The creek has changed its course," our mother would say, in a tone which implied terror and a sense of strangeness, as if a tragedy had been enacted.

We knew the moods of the creek, its levels of low-flow, half-high-flow, high-flow which all seemed to relate to interference at its source—the Reservoir. If one morning the water turned the color of clay and crowds of bubbles were passengers on every suddenly swift wave hurrying by, we would look at one another and remark with the fatality and reverence which attends a visitation or prophecy,

"The creek's going on high-flow. They must be doing something at the Reservoir."

By afternoon the creek would be on high-flow, turbulent, muddy, unable to be jumped across or paddled in or fished in, concealing beneath a swelling fluid darkness whatever evil which "they," the authorities, had decided to purge so swiftly and secretly from the Reservoir.

For so long, then, we obeyed our parents, and never walked as far as the Reservoir. Other things concerned us, other curiosities, fears, challenges. The school year ended. I got a prize, a large yellow book the color of cat's mess. Inside it were editions of newspapers, *The Worms' Weekly*, supposedly written by worms, snails, spiders. For the first part of the holidays we spent the time sitting in the long grass of our front lawn nibbling the stalks of shamrock and reading insect newspapers and relating their items to the lives of those living on our front lawn down among the summer-dry roots of the couch, tinkertailor, daisy, dandelion, shamrock, clover, and ordinary "grass." High summer came. The blowsy old red roses shed their petals to the regretful refrain uttered by our mother year after year at the same time, "I should have made potpourri, I have a wonderful recipe for potpourri in Dr. Chase's Book."

Our mother never made the potpourri. She merely quarreled with our father over how to pronounce it. The days became unbearably long and hot. Our Christmas presents were broken or too boring to care about. Celluloid dolls had loose arms and legs and rifts in their bright pink bodies; the invisible ink had poured itself out in secret messages; diaries frustrating in their smallness (two lines to a day) had been filled in for the whole of the coming year. ... Days at the beach were tedious, with no room in the bathing sheds so that we were forced to undress in the common room downstairs with its floor patched with wet and trailed with footmarks and sand and its tiny barred window (which made me believe that I was living in the French Revolution).

Rumors circled the burning world. The sea was drying up, soon you could paddle or walk to Australia. Sharks had been seen swimming inside the breakwater; one shark attacked a little boy and bit off his you-know-what.

We swam. We wore bathing togs all day. We gave up cowboys and ranches; and baseball and sledding; and "those games" where we mimicked grown-up life, loving and divorcing each other, kissing and slapping, taking secret paramours when our husband was working out of town. Everything exhausted us. Cracks appeared in the earth; the grass was bled yellow; the ground was littered with beetle shells and snail shells; flies came in from the unofficial rubbish-dump at the back of the house; the twisting flypapers hung from the ceiling; a frantic buzzing filled the room as the flypapers became crowded. Even the cat put out her tiny tongue, panting in the heat.

We realized, and were glad, that school would soon re-open. What was school like? It seemed so long ago, it seemed as if we had never been to school, surely we had forgotten everything we had learned, how frightening, thrilling and strange it would all seem! Where would we go on the first day, who would teach us, what were the names of the new books?

Who would sit beside us, who would be our best friend?

The earth crackled in early-autumn haze and still the February sun dried the world; even at night the rusty sheet of roofing-iron outside by the cellar stayed warm, but with rows of sweat-marks on it; the days were still long, with night face to face with morning and almost nothing in-between but a snatch of turning sleep with the blankets on the floor and the windows wide open to moths with their bulging lamplit eyes moving through the dark and their grandfather bodies knocking, knocking upon the walls.

Day after day the sun still waited to pounce. We were tired, our skin itched, our sunburn had peeled and peeled again, the skin on our feet was hard, there was dust in our hair, our bodies clung with the salt of sea-bathing and sweat, the towels were harsh with salt.

School soon, we said again, and were glad; for lessons gave shade to rooms and corridors; cloakrooms were cold and sunless. Then, swiftly, suddenly, disease came to the town. Infantile Paralysis. Black headlines in the paper, listing the number of cases, the number of deaths. Children everywhere, out in the country, up north, down south, two streets away.

The schools did not reopen. Our lessons came by post, in smudged print on rough white paper; they seemed make-shift and false, they inspired distrust, they could not com-pete with the lure of the sun still shining, swelling, the world would go up in cinders, the days were too long, there was nothing to do, there was nothing to do; the lessons were dull; in the front room with the navy-blue blind half down the window and the tiny splits of light showing through, and the lesson papers sometimes covered with unexplained blots of ink as if the machine which had printed them had broken down or rebelled, the lessons were even more dull.

Ancient Egypt and the flooding of the Nile!

The Nile, when we possessed a creek of our own with individual flooding!

"Well let's go along the gully, along by the creek," we would say, tired with all these.

Then one day when our restlessness was at its height, when the flies buzzed like bees in the flypapers, and the warped wood of the house cracked its knuckles out of boredom, the need for something to do in the heat, we found once again the only solution to our unrest.

Someone said, "What's the creek on?"

"Half-high flow."

"Good."

So we set out, in our bathing suits, and carrying switches of willow.

"Keep your sun hats on!" our mother called.

All right. We knew. Sunstroke when the sun clipped you over the back of the head, striking you flat on the ground. Sunstroke. Lightning. Even tidal waves were threatening us on this southern coast. The world was full of alarm.

"And don't go as far as the Reservoir!"

We dismissed the warning. There was enough to occupy us along the gully without our visiting the Reservoir. First, the couples. We liked to find a courting couple and follow them and when, as we knew they must do because they were tired or for other reasons, they found a place in the grass and lay down together, we liked to make jokes about them, amongst ourselves. "Just wait for him to kiss her," we would say. "Watch. There. A beaut. Smack."

Often we giggled and lingered even after the couple had observed us. We were waiting for them to do it. Every man and woman did it, we knew that for a fact. We speculated about technical details. Would he wear a frenchie? If he didn't wear a frenchie then she would start having a baby and be forced to get rid of it by drinking gin. Frenchies, by the way, were for sale in Woolworth's. Some said they were fingerstalls, but we knew they were frenchies and sometimes we would go downtown and into Woolworth's just to look at the frenchies for sale. We hung around the counter, sniggering. Sometimes we nearly died laughing, it was so funny.

After we tired of spying on the couples we would shout after them as we went our way.

> Pound, shillings and pence,
> a man fell over the fence,
> he fell on a lady,
> and squashed out a baby,
> pound, shillings and pence!

Sometimes a slight fear struck us—what if a man fell on us like that and squashed out a chain of babies?

Our other pastime along the gully was robbing the orchards, but this summer day the apples were small green hard and hidden by leaves. There were no couples either. We had the gully to ourselves. We followed the creek, whacking our sticks, gossiping and singing, but we stopped, immediately silent, when someone—sister or brother—said, "Let's go to the Reservoir!"

A feeling of dread seized us. We knew, as surely as we knew our names and our address Thirty-three Stour Street Ohau Otago South Island New Zealand Southern Hemisphere The World, that we would some day visit the Reservoir, but the time seemed almost as far away as leaving school, getting a job, marrying.

And then there was the agony of deciding the right time —how did one decide these things?

"We've been told not to, you know," one of us said timidly.

That was me. Eating bread and syrup for tea had made my hair red, my skin too, so that I blushed easily, and the grownups guessed if I told a lie.

"It's a long way," said my little sister.

"Coward!"

But it *was* a long way, and perhaps it would take all day and night, perhaps we would have to sleep there among the pine trees with the owls hooting and the old needle-filled warrens which now reached to the center of the earth where pools of molten lead bubbled, waiting to seize us if we tripped, and then there was the crying sound made by the trees, a sound of speech at its loneliest level where the meaning is felt but never explained, and it goes on and on in a kind of despair, trying to reach a point of understanding.

We knew that pine trees spoke in this way. We were lonely listening to them because we knew we could never help them to say it, whatever they were trying to say, for if the wind who was so close to them could not help them, how could we?

Oh no, we could not spend the night at the Reservoir among the pine trees.

"Billy Whittaker and his gang have been to the Reservoir,

Billy Whittaker and the Green Feather gang, one after-noon."

"Did he say what it was like?"

"No, he never said."

"He's been in an iron lung."

That was true. Only a day or two ago our mother had been reminding us in an ominous voice of the fact which roused our envy just as much as our dread, "Billy Whittaker was in an iron lung two years ago. Infantile paralysis."

Some people were lucky. None of us dared to hope that we would ever be surrounded by the glamour of an iron lung; we would have to be content all our lives with paltry flesh lungs.

"Well are we going to the Reservoir or not?"

That was someone trying to sound bossy like our father, —"Well am I to have salmon sandwiches or not, am I to have lunch at all today or not?"

We struck our sticks in the air. They made a whistling sound. They were supple and young. We had tried to make musical instruments out of them, time after time we hacked at the willow and the elder to make pipes to blow our music, but no sound came but our own voices. And why did two sticks rubbed together not make fire? Why couldn't we ever *make* anything out of the bits of the world lying about us?

An airplane passed in the sky. We craned our necks to read the writing on the underwing, for we collected air-plane numbers.

The plane was gone, in a glint of sun.

"Are we?" someone said.

"If there's an eclipse you can't see at all. The birds stop singing and go to bed."

"Well are we?"

Certainly we were. We had not quelled all our misgiving, but we set out to follow the creek to the Reservoir.

What is it? I wondered. They said it was a lake. I thought it was a bundle of darkness and great wheels which peeled and sliced you like an apple and drew you toward them with demonic force, in the same way that you were drawn beneath the wheels of a train if you stood too near the edge of the platform. That was the terrible danger when the Limited came rushing in and you had to approach to kiss arriving aunts.

We walked on and on, past wild sweet peas, clumps of cutty grass, horse mushrooms, ragwort, gorse, cabbage trees; and then, at the end of the gully, we came to strange territory, fences we did not know, with the barbed wire tearing at our skin and at our skirts put on over our bathing suits because we felt cold though the sun stayed in the sky.

We passed huge trees that lived with their heads in the sky, with their great arms and joints creaking with age and the burden of being trees, and their mazed and linked roots rubbed bare of earth, like bones with the flesh cleaned from them. There were strange gates to be opened or climbed over, new directions to be argued and plotted, notices which said TRESPASSERS WILL BE PROSECUTED BY ORDER. And there was the remote immovable sun shedding without gentleness its influence of burning upon us and upon the town, looking down from its heavens and considering our infantile-paralysis epidemic, and the children tired of holidays and wanting to go back to school with the new stiff books with their crackling pages, the scrubbed ruler with the sun rising on one side amidst the twelfths, tenths, millimeters, the new pencils to be sharpened with the pencil shavings flying in long pickets and light-brown curls scalloped with red or blue; the brown school, the bare floors, the clump clump in the corridors on wet days!

We came to a strange paddock, a bull-paddock with its occupant planted deep in the long grass, near the gate, a jersey bull polished like a wardrobe, burnished like copper, heavy beams creaking in the wave and flow of the grass.

"Has it got a ring through its nose? Is it a real bull or a steer?"

Its nose was ringed which meant that its savagery was tamed, or so we thought; it could be tethered and led; even so, it had once been savage and it kept its pride, unlike the steers who pranced and huddled together and ran like water through the paddocks, made no impression, quarried no massive shape against the sky.

The bull stood alone.

Had not Mr. Bennet been gored by a bull, his own tame bull, and been rushed to Glenham Hospital for thirty-three stitches? Remembering Mr. Bennet we crept cautiously close to the paddock fence, ready to escape.

Someone said, "Look, it's pawing the ground!"

A bull which pawed the ground was preparing for a charge. We escaped quickly through the fence. Then, plucking courage, we skirted the bushes on the far side of the paddock, climbed through the fence, and continued our walk to the Reservoir.

We had lost the creek between deep banks. We saw it now before us, and hailed it with more relief than we felt, for in its hidden course through the bull-paddock it had undergone change, it had adopted the shape, depth, mood of foreign water, foaming in a way we did not recognize as belonging to our special creek, giving no hint of its depth. It seemed to flow close to its concealed bed, not wishing any more to communicate with us. We realized with dismay that we had suddenly lost possession of our creek. Who had taken it? Why did it not belong to us any more? We hit our sticks in the air and forgot our dismay. We grew cheerful.

Till someone said that it was getting late, and we reminded one another that during the day the sun doesn't seem to move, it just remains pinned with a drawing pin against the sky, and then, while you are not looking, it suddenly slides down quick as the chopped-off head of a golden eel, into the sea, making everything in the world go dark.

"That's only in the tropics!"

We were not in the tropics. The divisions of the world in the atlas, the different colored cubicles of latitude and longitude fascinated us.

"The sand freezes in the desert at night. Ladies wear bits of sand. . . ."

"grains . . ."

"grains or bits of sand as necklaces, and the camels . . ."

"with necks like snails . . ."

"with horns, do they have horns?"

"Minnie Stocks goes with boys. . . ."

"I know who your boy is, I know who your boy is. . . ."

> Waiting by the garden gate,
> Waiting by the garden gate . . .

"We'll never get to the Reservoir!"

"Whose idea was it?"

"I've strained my ankle!"

Someone began to cry. We stopped walking.

"I've strained my ankle!"

There was an argument.

"It's not strained, it's sprained."

"strained."

"sprained."

"All right sprained then. I'll have to wear a bandage, I'll have to walk on crutches. . . ."

"I had crutches once. Look. I've got a scar where I fell off my stilts. It's a white scar, like a centipede. It's on my shins."

"Shins! Isn't it a funny word? Shins. Have you ever been kicked in the shins?"

"shins, funnybone . . ."

"It's humerus. . . ."

"knuckles . . ."

"a sprained ankle . . ."

"a strained ankle . . ."

"a whitlow, an ingrown toenail the roots of my hair warts spinal meningitis infantile paralysis . . ."

"Infantile paralysis, Infantile paralysis you have to be wheeled in a chair and wear irons on your legs and your knees knock together. . . ."

"Once you're in an iron lung you can't get out, they lock it, like a cage. . . ."

"You go in the amberlance . . ."

"*ambulance* . . ."

"amberlance . . ."

"ambulance to the hostible . . ."

"the *hospital,* an *amberlance to the hospital* . . ."

"Infantile Paralysis . . ."

"Friar's Balsam! Friar's Balsam!"

"Baxter's Lung Preserver, Baxter's Lung Preserver!"

"Syrup of Figs, California Syrup of Figs!"

"The creek's going on high-flow!"

Yes, there were bubbles on the surface, and the water was turning muddy. Our doubts were dispelled. It was the same old creek, and there, suddenly, just ahead, was a plantation of pine trees, and already the sighing sound of it reached our ears and troubled us. We approached it, staying close to the banks of our newly claimed creek, until once again the creek deserted us, flowing its own private course where we could not follow, and we found ourselves among the pine trees, a narrow strip of them, and beyond lay a vast surface of sparkling water, dazzling our eyes, its center chopped by tiny gray waves. Not a lake, nor a river, nor a sea.

"The Reservoir!"

The damp smell of the pine needles caught in our breath. There were no birds, only the constant sighing of the trees. We could see the water clearly now; it lay, except for the waves beyond the shore, in an almost perfect calm which we knew to be deceptive—else why were people so afraid of the Reservoir? The fringe of young pines on the edge, like toy trees, subjected to the wind, sighed and told us their sad secrets. In the Reservoir there was an appearance of neatness which concealed a disarray too frightening to be acknowledged except, without any defense, in moments of deep sleep and dreaming. The little sparkling innocent waves shone now green, now gray, petticoats, lettuce leaves; the trees sighed, and told us to be quiet, hush-sh, as if something were sleeping and should not be disturbed—perhaps that was what the trees were always telling us, to hush-sh in case we disturbed something which must never ever be awakened?

What was it? Was it sleeping in the Reservoir? Was that why people were afraid of the Reservoir?

Well we were not afraid of it, oh no, it was only the Reservoir, it was nothing to be afraid of, it was just a flat Reservoir with a fence around it, and trees, and on the far side a little house (with wheels inside?), and nothing to be afraid of.

"The Reservoir, The Reservoir!"

A noticeboard said DANGER, RESERVOIR.

Overcome with sudden glee we climbed through the fence and swung on the lower branches of the trees, shouting at intervals, gazing possessively and delightedly at the sheet of water with its wonderful calm and menace,

"The Reservoir! The Reservoir! The Reservoir!"

We quarreled again about how to pronounce and spell the word.

Then it seemed to be getting dark—or was it that the trees were stealing the sunlight and keeping it above their heads? One of us began to run. We all ran, suddenly, wildly, not caring about our strained or sprained ankles, through the trees out into the sun where the creek, but it was our creek no longer, waited for us. We wished it were our creek, how we wished it were our creek! We had lost all account of time. Was it nearly night? Would darkness overtake us, would we have to sleep on the banks of the creek that did not belong to us any more, among the wild sweet peas and the tussocks and the dead sheep? And would the eels come up out of the creek, as people said they did, and on their travels through the paddocks would they change into people who would threaten us and bar our way, TRESPASSERS WILL BE PROSECUTED, standing arm in arm in their black glossy coats, swaying, their mouths open, ready to swallow us? Would they ever let us go home, past the orchards, along the gully? Perhaps they would give us Infantile Paralysis, perhaps we would never be able to walk home, and no one would know where we were, to bring us an iron lung with its own special key!

We arrived home, panting and scratched. How strange! The sun was still in the same place in the sky!

The question troubled us, "Should we tell?"

The answer was decided for us. Our mother greeted us as we went in the door with, "You haven't been long away, kiddies. Where have you been? I hope you didn't go anywhere near the Reservoir."

Our father looked up from reading his newspapers. "Don't let me catch you going near the Reservoir!"

We said nothing. How out-of-date they were! They were actually afraid!

prizes

Life is hell, but at least there are prizes. Or so one thought. One knew of the pit ahead, of the grownups lying there rewarded, arranged, and faded, who were so long ago bright as poppies. One learned to take one's own deserved place on the edge, ready to leap, not to hang back in a status-free huddle where bodies were warm together and the future darkness seemed less frightening. Therefore, one learned to win prizes, to be surrounded in sleep by a dream of ordinal numbers, to stand in best clothes upon platforms in order to receive medals threaded upon black-and-gold ribbons, books "bound in calf," scrolled certificates. One's face became, from habit, incandescent with achievement.

I had my share of prizes, and of resentment when nobody recognized my efforts; for instance, year after year, when the New Zealand Agricultural and Pastoral Society held its show in the Onui Drill Hall, I made a buttonhole of a rose and a sprig of maidenhair fern tied together with raffia, which I entered for the Flower Display, Gentleman's Buttonhole. It was never displayed, and it never won a prize. One morning, a militant woman in a white coat made a speech to the whole school from the front steps, before Bertie Dowling played the kettledrum for us to march inside, and in her speech the woman accused too many people of entering for the Buttonhole Section, and advised us not to try to make buttonholes, as they were an art beyond our years that even grownups found difficult to master. "It has never been explained," the woman said, "why so many children enter buttonholes in the Flower Show." (Bertie Dowling had the sticks raised, ready to play the drum. He was very clever at it; he was a small, sunburned, wiry boy with long feet like a rabbit.)

I felt antagonistic toward the woman visitor. Who was she to order me not to make buttonholes for the Flower Show? I persisted, as I say, year after year, yet always, once I had surrendered my exhibit, neat in its little box cadged from the jeweler's, I never heard of it again. I had so much determination and so little wisdom that I never grasped the futility of my struggle, although I realized that when talents were being devised and distributed my name was not included in the short list of those blessed with the power to make gentlemen's buttonholes that would reach the display table at the Flower Show in the Drill Hall and win First, Second, or Third Prize.

I won six and fourpence for handwriting. At that time, I was in love with my parents; therefore, I decided to buy my mother a best-china cup, saucer, and plate with the entire six and fourpence, even though at that time I also had a fondness for Sante Chocolate Bars, jelly beans, and chocolate fish whose insides were a splurge of pink rubbery substance with tiny air holes in it. When I gave my mother the best-china cup, saucer, and plate she said, "You shouldn't have," and, wrapping the set carefully in tissue paper, she placed it in the sideboard cupboard with the other dishes that we never used—not even for the banquet to see the New Year in—like the gravy boat, the tiny cream jug with the picture of a Dutch girl, the vegetable dishes with the picture of a rooster crowing on each one. Then my mother locked the door. I never saw her using the cup, saucer, and plate. It was best china, too, the man in Peak's told me. My mother always said she was keeping the set for when she could *really* use it, drinking out of the cup, resting a silver spoon in the saucer, tasting (with a cake fork) a slice of marble cake upon the plate. Although I could not then discern the difference between using something and *really* using it, there was evidently a distinction so important that when my mother died she had still not been able to use, really to use, my six-and-fourpenny gift to her.

My next prize was for a poem that revealed both my lack of scientific knowledge and my touching disbelief in change by concluding with the lines

> And till the sky falls from above,
> These things of nature I shall love.

Uncle Ted, of my favorite wireless station in Christchurch, read my poem over the air, between a recording of "The Nutcracker, Waltz of the Flowers," and the fifth episode of *David and Dawn in Fairyland*, and two days later I received through the post an order for ten shillings, with part of which I bought for myself an unsatisfactory diary and a John Bull Printing Set, which I used, printing my name, and rude rhymes, and insults to the rest of the family, until the ink dried on the navy-blue pad; the remainder of the ten shillings I saved in a Post Office Bank, which could not be opened unless it was taken to the Post Office. I broke into it with a kitchen knife when my bathing cap perished and the weather was warm enough for swimming.

Prizes. They arrived unexpectedly, or I waited greedily for them at the end of every school year, when I received one or two, sometimes three, books with the school motto, "Pleasure from Work," inscribed on the flyleaf beneath the cramped, detailed writing of the form mistress setting out the reasons for my prize. Reasons were necessary, for no school had yet learned to distribute prizes at random, first come, first served, in the manner that my mother had adopted, in exasperation, when she was pestered for raisins, dates, or the last of the chocolate biscuits. I collected so many books: *Treasure Island; Silas Marner; Emma; Poems of Longfellow*, with a heart-throbbing picture of Hiawatha bearing Minnehaha across the river:

> Over wide and rushing rivers
> In his arms he bore the maiden;

India, with illustrations colored as if with cochineal; *Boys and Girls Who Became Famous;* and—during the war, when books were scarce—a musty old rained-on and stained volume of poems about blossoms, barns, and wine presses, printed in tall, dark type, where snakes lurked in every capital letter.

Prizes. Some did not get prizes. Dotty Baker with the greasy hair never got a prize. Maud Gray, who found it hard to read even simple sentences aloud, never got a prize.

Maud Gray! She was the stodgiest girl in the class; all the teachers made fun of her, and most of the pupils, including myself, followed their example. Her eyes were brittle and brown, like cracked acorn shells; her face was pale and blotched, like milk on the turn.

Years later, I was visiting Onui. I was walking desolately in the rain along the main street, wearing my dirty old gabardine and my dowdy clothes and feeling fifteen instead of twenty-five, when, just beyond the bed of poppies in the center of the street, I saw two beautiful women wheeling prams, and their proud gait was so noticeable I tried to recall when and where I had seen before that superior parading of the victorious. And then I realized that I had walked onto the platform in the same way, year after year, to receive my prizes. Dotty Baker, Maud Gray! As they passed with their cocooned, quilted, embroidered treasure, I could not even assert my superiority by whispering, "You cheated in history, you couldn't learn poetry by heart, you never had your name in the paper. . . . First in geometry, French, English, history. . . ."

They smiled at me and I smiled at them. We shared the pit, each in her place. The rain poured upon the bed of crushed poppies between us. Yet the delicacy and distance of the two women were unmistakable; I grudged their proud cloaks as they trooped, clients of love, on their specially reserved side of the world. But—prizes. They never won prizes. My only retaliation was prizes—listing them, remembering.

I wrote to a children's newspaper, sending poems that were awarded ten or five or three marks. When I had earned one hundred marks, I received the usual prize of two guineas. For one guinea my father bought me a tennis racket, as he said, "on the cheap," but when he showed it to me I was alarmed to discover that the strings were black instead of white, and the name was unfamiliar—Double Duke. I was the loneliest person in the world with my black-stringed Double Duke. Why had my father not realized that every other girl at school possessed a white-stringed Vantage? Ah, it was sad enough to have an old wireless at home with a name no one had heard of and with tubes so few in number compared with the tubes in other sets. The conversations in class went: "Have you got a wireless at home? How many tubes?" The prestige of owning things mattered so much, and to have a tennis racket with a strange name and grotesque strings was punishment indeed. I was so ashamed of my tennis racket that I seldom used it.

With my other guinea from the newspaper I had the unexpected fortune to be chosen by Hessie Sutton, a woman up the road, as her pupil for music lessons—the piano—at a reduced rate, and every Tuesday and Friday after school I claimed an hour of Hessie Sutton's time in the front room of the house where she lived with her mother and a white parrot whose perpetual screaming inspired complaining letters to the evening paper.

The front room was large and carpeted, with sparkling, bubble-shaped windows. The piano made wonderfully clean sounds as the keys sank into and sprang from their green bedding; the sounds filled me with a polished sense of opulence and cleanliness, and each note emerged bravely and milkily alone and poured into me, up to my neck. I swallowed. I liked Hessie Sutton's piano. We had none at home. At my aunt's house, where I went to practice once a week, there was an old piano with soapy yellow keys that stuck halfway, and the lower or upper half of each sound had been weathered down so that each note came forth deprived, diseased, with an invalid petulance and stricture.

"But you must not bite your nails," Hessie Sutton warned me. "You will never be able to play the piano if you bite your nails!" That was my first intimation that Hessie Sutton was a spy. I clenched my fists, hiding my fingernails.

At school, I said, "I learn music, do you?" Dotty Baker, Maud Gray, and others learned music, but mostly they were like uncooked pastry at it; they suffered a dearth of warmth, expansion, gold finish. On the cold June days, when the Music Festival was held, we sat miserably in the hall, our coats over our knees, listening to a "Marche Militaire" being played by schoolgirl dentists and carpenters.

My first piece was named "Puck." I went down to the stationer's to by it on tick, and the ginger-haired boy served me, and his face had a rust-colored blush, like a dock leaf in autumn, because he had to go to the small room at the back of the shop and ask his parents if it would be all right to serve me, as our bill had not been paid. On my way home with "Puck," I met Hessie Sutton and smiled at her, shyly and excitedly, but when she glanced at the parcel under my arm and the music half wrapped, and gave an understanding smile, my face clouded in a fierce frown. How dare she see me and divine my excitement! How dare she! How I hated her!

That afternoon, when I went for my lesson, she heightened my sense of shame. "I saw you." She pounced as soon as I entered the room. "I saw you," she said, like a detective giving evidence, "coming home with your new piece of music. I guessed how excited you were!"

"I wasn't caring at all," I said sullenly.

"Yes, you were," Hessie Sutton insisted. "I saw it in your face! I *knew!*"

I did not understand why she should appear so triumphant, as if by seizing on a momentary aspect of my behavior she had uncovered a life of deceit in me. Why, she honked with triumph like the soldier who brought back the golden horn from the underworld as proof of the secret activities of the twelve dancing princesses! I did not realize that people's actions are mysteries that are so seldom solved.

"I knew, I knew!" Hessie Sutton kept saying as I sat down to try out "Puck."

From that day, I no longer enjoyed my music lessons. I was weary of being spied upon. People were saying, observing me closely, "She's filling out, she's growing tall, look at her hair, isn't that Grace's chin she's got, and there's no doubting where her smile comes from!"

You see how derivative I was made out to be? Nothing belonged to me, not even my body, and now with Hessie Sutton and her spying ways I could not call my feelings my own. Why did people have so much need to stake their claim in other people? Were they scared of the bailiffs' arriving in their own house? I stopped learning music. I was in despair. I could no longer use prizes as a fortress. In spite of my books bound in calf, my scrolled certificates, the prize essay on the Visit to the Flour Mill, and my marks of merit in the children's newspaper, I was being invaded by people who wanted *their* prizes from *me*.

And now I lie in the pit, finally arranged, faded, robbed of all prizes, while still under every human sky the crows wheel and swoop, dividing, dividing the spoils of the dead.

a sense of proportion

The sun's hair stood on end. The sky accommodated all visiting darkness and light. Leaves were glossy green, gold, brown, dried, dead and bleached in drifts beneath the trees. Snow fell in all seasons, white hyphens dropping evenly, linking syllables of sky and earth. Flowers bloomed forever, spinning their petal-spokes like golden wheels, sucking the sun like whirlpools. Black-polished, brick-dusted, spotted ladybirds big as airplanes with pleated wings like sky-wide curtains parting, flew home to flame and cinders.

Houses had pointed roofs of red and yellow with tall chimneys emitting scribbles of pale blue smoke. All houses had gardens around them, paths with parallel sides enclosing pebbles; gates were five-barred, with children swinging from them. The children wore red stockings. They had ribbons tied in their hair. Their eyes were round and blue, their eyebrows were arched, their lips were rosy. Their hands displayed five fingers for all to see, their feet pointed the same way, left or right, in gaudy shoes with high heels. The ocean was filled with sailing boats, the sky was filled with rainbows, suns, scalloped clouds.

Coats had many buttons, intricate collars with lace edges. The bricks of houses were carefully outlined. Front doors had four panels and a knocker in its exact position.

Winds were visible, fat men or witches with puffed cheeks in the four corners of the sky. The trees leaned with their skirts up over their heads.

The streets were full of painted rubber balls divided carefully into bright colors.

Men wore hats placed firmly upon their heads.

Dogs walked, their tails like masts in the air.

Cats had mile-long whiskers like rays of the sun. They sat, their tails curled about them, containing them. Their ears were pricked, forever listening.

The moon, like the sun, had a face, a smile, eyes, teeth. The moon journeyed on a cloud convoyed by elaborately five-pointed stars.

There was no distance or shade in our infant drawing. Everything loomed close to the eye; rainbows in the heavens could be clutched as securely as the few blades of bright green grass (the color of strong lemonade) growing symmetrically in the lower right-hand corner of the picture.

Some years passed during which we learned to draw and paint from a small tin of Reeve's Water Colors: Chinese White, Gamboge Tint, Indigo, Yellow Ochre (which I pronounced and believed to be *Yellow Ogre*) Burnt Sienna: the names gave excitement, pain, wonder. We were shown how to paint a sunset in the exact gradations of color, to make a blue water-color sky, a scientific rainbow (Read

Over Your Greek Book In Verse) receding into the distance. The teacher placed an apple and a pear in a glass bowl upon the table. We drew them, making careful shading, painstakingly coloring the autumn tints of the apple. We did not paint the worm inside it.

We drew vases of flowers, autumn scenes, furniture which existed merely to cast a perfect shadow to be portrayed by a B.B. pencil. The Art lessons were long and tedious. I could never get my shadow or my distance correct. My rainbows and paths would not recede, and my furniture, my boats at anchor, my buildings stood flat upon the page, all in a total clamor of foreground.

"You must draw things," said Miss Collins the Art Teacher, "as they seem. Notice the way the path narrows as it approaches the foothills."

"But it is the same breadth all the way!"

"No," Miss Collins insisted. "You must learn to draw these tricks of the eye. You must learn to think in terms of them."

I never learned to draw tricks of the eye. My paint refused to wash in the correct proportion when I was trying to fill the paper sky with sunrises, sunsets, and rainbows. My garden spades were without strength or shape; their shadows stayed unowned, apart, incredible, more like stray tatters shed from a profusion of dark remnants of objects. My vases had no depth, and their flowers withered in their laborious journey from the table to the page of my scholastic Drawing Book Number Three.

The classroom was dusty and hot and there was the soft buzz of talking, and people walking to and fro getting fresh water and washing brushes; and Miss Collins touring the aisles, giving gentle but insistent advice about colors and shadows. Her hair was in plaits, wound close to her head.

In moments of calm or boredom the fact or fancy rippled about the classroom, lapping at our curiosity, Miss Collins wears a wig. Once, long ago, in the days of the Spartans and Athenians, someone had observed Miss Collins in the act of removing her wig.

"She is quite bald," the rumor went.

Like so many of the other teachers Miss Collins lived with her mother in a little house, a woven spider's nest with the leaves and rain closing in, just at the edge of town. She cherished a reputation as a local painter and at most exhibitions you could see her poplar trees, tussock scenes, mountains, lakes, all in faded colors, with sometimes in the corner, or looking out of the window of a decayed farmhouse, the tiny fierce black lines that were the shape of people.

Every term she gave us examinations which were days of flurry and anxiety when we filed into the Art Room and took our places at the bare desks and gazed with respectful awe at the incongruous display on the table—fruit, a vase of flowers, perhaps a kettle or similar utensil whose shape would strain our ability to "match sides." And for the next forty minutes our attention would be fixed upon the clutter of objects, the submissive Still Life which yet huddled powerfully before us, preying upon us with its overlapping corners and sides and deceptive shadows.

How I envied Leila Smith! Leila Smith could draw perfect kettles, rainbows, cupboards. Her pictures always showed the exact number of strokes of rain, when rain fell, and snowflakes when the scene required them. By instinct Leila Smith *knew*. On those days when the gods attended the classroom, penetrating the dust-layered windows hung with knotted cords so complicated that a special Window Monitor was needed to operate them, and the window sills ranged with dead flowers and beans in water—when the gods walked up and down the aisles at our Art Examination they showed extra care for Leila Smith, they guided her hand across the page. When they passed my desk, alas, they vindictively jogged my elbow. Miss Collins despaired of ever teaching me.

"How's your drawing?" my father would say, who had spent the winter evenings painting in oils from a tiny cigarette card the ship that carried him to the First World War. His sisters painted as well; their work hung in the passage—roses, dogs, clouded ladies, and one storm at sea.

"I can't draw," I said. "I can't paint."

Miss Collins readily agreed with me. "Your perspective and proportion are well below average. Your shading is poor."

The obsession with shading fascinated me. All things, even kettles and fire shovels, stood under the sun complete and unique with their shadows, fighting to preserve them. It was an act of charity for us to draw the shadow with as much love (frustration, despair) as we gave to drawing the shape itself. In the world of Miss Collins, morning and evening were perpetual, with the shadows spread beautifully alongside each object, their contours matching perfectly, a mirror image of the body. Why was it that in my world the sun stood everlastingly at noon; objects were stripped of their shadows, forced to stand in brilliant light, alone?

In the end Miss Collins gave up trying to teach me to draw and paint. She spent her time giving hints to Leila Smith. Oh how wonderful were Leila's flowers and fire shovels, garden spades and kettles!

Sometimes Miss Collins would ask us to paint things "out of our head."

It showed, she said, whether we had any imagination.

I had no imagination. My poverty could not even provide

shadows or proportionate rainbows. The paths in my head stayed the same width right to the foothills and over the mountains which were no obstacles to vision, as mountains are agreed to be; they were transparent mountains, and there was the path, the same width as before, annihilating distance, at last disappearing only at the boundary of the picture.

Distance did not cloud the outline of objects; trees were not blurred; you could count the leaves upon the trees, even on the slopes of the mountain you could count the pine needles hanging in their green brushes.

Yes, it was true; I had no sense of proportion.

When I last saw Miss Collins she had been taken to the hospital after a stroke, and was lying quietly in the hospital bed. She was dying. The torment of the unshaded world lay before her, the sun in her sky stood resolutely at noon, her life was out of proportion, there was no distance, the foreground blazed with looming and light.

She closed her eyes and died.

Her life, in its spider's web, had absorbed her. She had been aided, comforted, made less lonely, by acknowledging and yielding to a trick of the eye. How does one learn to accept that trick and its blessings before it is too late, before the shadows are razed and the sun stands pitiless at perpetual noon?

royal icing

My mother had no money and no clothes except for an old sack tied around her waist, and a costume, with moth balls in the pockets, hanging in the front wardrobe. Her titties were flat and heavy against her tummy. Her legs had varicose veins. Her forehead was damp with steam or sweat or something which, sighing and waving her powerful arms in the humid air, she called "atmosphere."

"The atmosphere's very heavy today," she would remark. "It's something in the atmosphere that is responsible."

Responsibility was a terrible substance to be apportioned, and mostly it came to rest upon the government; but the atmosphere could accept it just as well.

With so much, then, in the atmosphere, why did my mother want to bother with a set of icing-forcers?

She was a poor housekeeper, people said.

She was soft, they said.

We knew. We banged on the bedroom wall, "Mum, bring us a piece!"

She brought us a piece of bread and jam.

We tore the wallpaper and poked our fingers through the scrim, looking for secret documents. We ripped the inside from the cupboard, looking for secret panels. We broke the locks on the door, trying to be burglars. We climbed on the roof and bent the spouting. We kept dogs which fussed about us with wet noses, and my father scratched for fleas in the night, keeping a torch by the bed to save electricity, and leaping up and down at all hours crying, "Got one, Got one, Hear them Crack?"

He lay the dead fleas in a row on the washstand, to compare each night's tally the following morning. It did not seem possible that so many fleas could have come to live in our house; they did not know evidently that our house was haunted in the shower in the bathroom where a former tenant had cut his throat with a razor. Or perhaps fleas were not concerned with such details.

And still, twice a year, Christmas and New Year, the cakes were baked and there was no icing-forcer to write professional greetings upon them or arrange the icing in patterns of leaves and petals.

"I tell you what," my father said one day as he watched my mother icing the Christmas cake. "We need a set of those things, you know, they use them for icing cakes."

"One of these days," my mother said. "We never know, do we, one of these days?"

"Who knows?" my father said.

That was a mysterious conversation. My father gave it up and settled down again to sew the straps on his workbag, for he believed in making his own workbag; while my mother continued icing the cake, dipping the knife in hot water and spreading, coaxing, trying not to mind when the stuff ran down the sides of the cake and the pink icing flowed into the white.

And so our lives continued and we did not think that fact mysterious because we expected it; aunts, uncles, grandparents, people over the road or in the next street were for dying in the end but we were for being alive; with so many fat spaniel dogs lying down in the corner of the washhouse to have puppies, we had no choice.

The fleas were such a worry. What if they spread to the neighbors? Not all my father's cleverness could get rid of them. And my father was very clever. He sewed and painted pictures on velvet cushion covers, he painted in oils, he dug beautiful double depths in the garden to plant the potatoes, he danced the Highland Fling and the Sword Dance and a dance where he sang

I'd rather have a hard-boiled egg,
I'd rather have a hard-boiled egg;

he could play the bagpipes and sing "Ragtime Cowboy Joe." But still he did not earn enough money to buy a set of icing-forcers in order to write greetings on the Christmas and New Year cakes.

"They're like guns," my mother said dreamily. "You can use them for shooting out biscuit dough into any shape you want."

"You'll need to keep them clean," my father warned her.

My mother was not expert at cleaning, she was not interested in sweeping four corners of a room and peering under the mat to surprise the dust-in-hiding. No. She stood at the back door and stared at the sunset over Weston, Waiareka, and Wainakarua, and sighed.

"Oh, oh," I said to myself, "what do you need to be happy?"

I longed for happiness and complete satisfaction.

Yet there wasn't a mincer in the house! How could anyone be happy without a mincer? Something had broken in our old mincer, and anyway the parts were lost and rusted and the main body of it was lying in a corner of the wash house beside the firewood, the old *Free Lance* magazines, and cast-out envelopes full of useless Tatts Results. I gave up hope of ever again having a mincer and being able to watch the mince coming out bright red with white flecks into the dish. I had given up longing for so many things which I desperately needed—long straight hair kept in place by a clasp or ribbon, a film test to get me to Hollywood where I would sing, amazing everyone, *"Oh the days are gone since beauty bright my heart's chain wore,"* and,

> *I had a pal Blackie so dear to my heart,*
> *but the warders they shot him . . ."*

an everlasting ticket to the pictures, dancing lessons, the bills all paid, a different mother in a white dress, a father who did not keep saying, in spite of his cleverness, "You'll feel the back of my hand in a moment," "I'll warm your bottom if I get hold of you. . . ." So many needs.

It was true that we had a separator which whined and trembled and vibrated, and I would stand on a chair and pour the foamy new milk into the bowl at the top. The bowl was a most beautiful shape, containing, generous, and even if the cows were in full milk the bowl never overflowed. I used to watch the skim milk pouring, spurting from the silver-colored tube, and the cream dripping in fat blobs into the jug on the other side.

"Skim milk!" my mother said in horror. "Never drink skim milk!"

I used to pat the butter together with the scrubbed ribbed butter pats.

So. A separator, an old mincer—were they enough to guarantee happiness?

Also, I had a possie of my own under the silver birch trees. I had a pet cockabully which I had tamed myself, and which came when I called it, although it had no choice because it lived in a restricted area and just happened to be near.

But these were not enough. It seemed that nothing was ever enough.

Year after year my mother said, "We need a set of those things that bakers use to ice their cakes."

And year after year my father agreed.

"It would be nice, dandy in fact," he said. "We do need a new mincer as well, you know."

For a short time of suspense there was declared competition between the superiority of a mincer and a set of icing-forcers; neither won. Whenever my father wanted Shepherd's Pie for dinner the meat was chopped by hand, and when Christmas and New Year came the cakes were iced without the adroit targeting of an icing-forcer.

We grew up. We left school and home and sent sudden telegrams during the week, ARRIVING MIDNIGHT TRAIN. There was something at home which we expected to find during the weekend, something which had haunted us while we were absent, enticed us with images of peace and comfort; yet, strangely, when we had left the Midnight Express and made our way home and had our cup of hot cocoa and gone tiptoe to our room with its musty smell and its shelves of already worm-attended books, we knew a feeling of disillusionment, of having been cheated. The something was as out of our reach as the new mincer, the set of icing-forcers.

My father retired, with a dinner set as a present.

My mother's hair went white, suddenly, as if she had been

shocked in the night by a presence which was revealed to her alone; no one knew its identity; she was acquainted with more things in the atmosphere than we dreamed of.

Then one day my father arrived home with a parcel which he opened on the kitchen table.

"See," he said, and spilled the metal parts from their cardboard box onto the oilcloth. "See, you can use it for writing on cakes, for arranging the dough of biscuits, remember how we've always wanted it?"

My mother gazed in admiration. "So many parts!" she exclaimed, and proceeded to count them. "Why, there must be about ten! And all different! Of course I don't make cakes every day, and now that the children aren't home . . ."

"But at Christmas, and New Year, and for visitors. Just look," my father said, taking each part separately and holding it up to the light, like a bank clerk testing money to decide if it were counterfeit or genuine. He twirled the parts, gently, protectively, like coins, upon the table, listening carefully. "Look. Perfect."

Then his face became serious and stern. "They'll have to be cleaned thoroughly after use," he said. "And dried on the rack above the fire. We don't want them getting rusty, like the mincer, or stuck with scum, like the separator."

"No of course not," my mother said, looking guilty and afraid.

After all, a set of icing-forcers was a grave responsibility, and now that she was growing older she was finding it more difficult to perform the agility known as "coping" which I had long fancied to mean creeping up to one's enemies, unsuspected, and enveloping them in a dark cloth, perhaps smothering them.

My mother had a natural difficulty in coping.

With the icing set there seemed to be so many parts, so

many complicated instructions printed in the leaflet, and all merely to write Merry Christmas, Happy New Year upon two cakes to make them appear as if they had been baked at the baker's!

Christmas came. The cake was baked, and when it had cooled my mother iced it the old way, dipping a knife in hot water, and plowing the icing like a field of snow across the top of the cake.

"You never used the icing set," my father accused.

My mother flushed guiltily. "Well," she said, hesitating.

"You might have used them," my father persisted. "It's only twice a year."

"I think though the old way's best," my mother said. "The icing set is all right for bakers."

She was thoughtful a moment.

"Couldn't we exchange them?"

My father looked horrified. "After all these years! Isn't it what we've always wanted? No. It's true what you say, Mum, they're not really much use."

But they did not exchange them. Both my mother and my father appreciated the set. Sometimes when it was my father's habit to bring out the Postcards he had brought back from the War, his book of fishing flies, or back numbers of the *Railway Magazine*, he would fetch the icing set as well, taking it from its cardboard box and spilling the parts upon the table where he would carefully handle each one, as if he were a collector perusing valuable stamps or coins.

My mother gave the icing set a special place on the sideboard beside the few pieces of china which were too good to be used and the pair of little blue glass slippers which had been sent with Auntie Maggie's things when she died, and which now housed buttons, domes, needles, hooks and eyes.

But the icing set was never used. It became a landmark on the sideboard.

"It's behind the icing set."

"It's to the left of the icing set."

"It's just in front of the icing set."

And my mother and father were growing old without ever writing festive messages upon the Christmas and New Year cakes!

My mother was afraid of Death. She saw Death sometimes. He would be bending over the coal in the coal house, or in the garden tying up the broad beans or the sweet peas that had strayed from their trellis. Sometimes he sat in the sun with his hands in his lap, snoring. He could afford to snore. And still the icing set stayed on the sideboard next to the best china and the little blue glass slippers, and between my mother and my father on one side, and Death on the other there was a diminishing gulf to be filled or concealed in some way; the years of their lives were like a slowly closing wound where the edges must be prevented at all costs from uniting.

What dreams were left for them now to wedge between birth and death?

Perhaps to stretch life, like a tightening shoe, to make it fit for ever and ever?

Tell me, what do we need? What dream must we pursue and not be afraid to grasp and possess when it finally becomes reality? Is it better to want and get an icing-forcer, a mincer, than to walk for the remainder of our lives about the house with a little dagger in our pocket trying to catch Death bending over the coal in the coal house or tying up the stray broad beans or sweet peas on the trellis, or sitting in the sun snoring? Trying to catch and kill him, and then, with a surprised look on our face, turning the dagger to our own heart?

obstacles

Poetic justice has it that way.

The track to the Zig-Zag was arrived at by crossing the creek at the foot of the hill. At one end of the creek there was a wooden plank used as a bridge; at the other end there was a thick licorice-colored ribbed pipe which carried, they said, water, sewage, or arms and legs torn from people in the sudden gales that raved through the gorge from the high country and that, blinded with snow, were unable to distinguish trees from people, nor is there much difference as they all beat their foreheads and stand stock-still in moonlight with their skin glittering. Yet no one really discovered what the pipe contained, although at one time a leak sprang in the side, but a growth of moss made a nest there, hiding the nature of what flowed out, and with all the secret flowing the area of the town, the plains, the back-country bush was combed for Dutch Boys, we children being in Standard Two and being fed History with startling tales of courage and roses in floods and wars.

Now you would imagine that if you wished to climb the Zig-Zag and sit on the seat and stare down at the shimmeringly contained town with its skirt of leaves and red pompon chimneys, that you would naturally (they say "naturally as breathing" which is the first unnatural imposition) walk across the conventional wooden plank. If a wooden plank is laid there for you why not walk upon it?

Why?

Although the plank sagged in the middle and was split by sunlight and the shadeless inquisitions of noon, it was entirely safe. People had faith in it. Grownups walked upon it. The water beneath it was shallow, dribbling harmlessly over the humpbacked stones and the flat oblong ones, blessed and white like pillows. Who would drown if they fell from the wooden plank?

But at the other end of the creek, beneath the pipe, the water was so deep that rumors labeled it unfathomable, like Lake Waihola, and no one could tell from gazing in at the silvered logs and festering weeds that tangled above the eel-dark mysteries, whether the rumors were true. Also, if you searched in the wilderness of grass near the pipe you could find a faded wooden notice printed with the word DANGER. Something or someone temporal, human, climatic, had erased the *D*. The notice now spelled ANGER.

People who braved this warning and crossed the creek by way of the pipe became admired, envied. We all wanted to be admired, envied. The world was divided into children who had walked over the pipe, and the remaining cowardy-custards who sullenly scuffed their toes along the footpath, hung their heads in shame, or tried to feign total absorption in acquiring stars at hopscotch. Was it not better—more expedient—to sign one's name within a chalked star upon the footpath beneath the cool shade of sycamore trees crackling their brittle biscuit-colored windmills, than to fall, trying to walk across the pipe, and be seized and gobbled by eels or dragged under to the bottomless pit?

But dreams and longings ignore expediency. The thought of the pipe dominated our waking and sleeping lives. At mealtimes we no longer talked of lessons or games or people who had got the strap at school or had cheated or wet on the seats or whose mothers had visited with excuses and certificates. We did not tease one another at the table, or flick bread crumbs while our father was looking the other way, or kick ankles. No one put the treacle spoon in my curly hair, by accident. We children were serious and absorbed.

"Tony Flett has walked across the pipe," someone would say, in a tone of challenge and envy. Tony Flett or Jack Hunt or Bluey Conway. Or Phyllis Webb. Phyllis Webb, whose big sister Dorry was skinny and tottered on high heels and her lips were smeared with poppy juice and she dipped her face in the flour bag! None of us had yet walked the pipe. Day and night I dreamed of it. Several times I had begun, pressing my sandals upon the slippery surface, trying to find a toe hold in the patterns of ribbing, but always after the first few steps I had flung out my arms, wobbled my body this way and that, and finally retreated, yelling, to the safety of the bank. Once I think, or perhaps I dreamed it, not being able in dreams to accomplish the seemingly impossible, I crawled across the pipe. But crawling did not count. You had to walk, slowly, with arrogance and composure. Your glory was enhanced if you stopped in the middle of your journey and facing the spectators (who were necessary as witnesses since formal proof was always demanded on the principle that all things must be proved) remarked casually that it was all so easy, so easy, that you could set up camp there, halfway across the creek and not be in the least disturbed, that really you couldn't think why you had waited so long before walking across the pipe. And when you approached the other side of the creek there was to be no sudden leap to safety, but still the same calm bearing and unworried expression which said, See, it's easy. You know that I could hurry now, at the end; but why hurry; how dignified I am! The whole thing is as safe as houses!

Yet if walking across the pipe was as safe as houses why didn't everybody do it, why was the world so surely divided into the strong and the weak, the brave and the cowardy-custards? Safe as houses? Were houses safe, after all? With gusts of paternal anger flapping the wallpaper and trying to lift the roof? With tedious habitual beetles making railway lines in the foundations of love, leaving small cargoes of sawdust on the platform for people to taste and find in their mouths in the morning and spit out in ritual circles down bathroom sinks, in gutters, in the alpine crevices of clutched handkerchiefs?

Day by day the strong became more numerous, the number of the weak diminished. If you had tried and failed you remained among the weak; you could obtain no glory from the fact that you had at least tried.

Soon the whole world talked of nothing but crossing the pipe. Surely it was in the newspapers, on the front pages, the middle and back pages? Wasn't it discussed in parliament? People in the street, on corners, downtown on a Friday night, in shops, offices, everywhere they were talking about crossing the pipe. Or so it seemed.

Prowess in other activities no longer had meaning. No one

was impressed by your boast that you had skipped a class at school, that you had been let out early for having ten out of ten in sums, that you could get through bounce-up-and-down-claps-backward-and-forward at baseball without missing. Possessions human or material no longer gave you prestige or ensured that you would be surrounded by friends, invited to parties, taken to other little girl's homes and introduced as "My best friend, she's got a dolls' house," or "My best friend, she's got an aunt who's an aunt on the wireless too." Things of accepted value were drained of importance. Who cared if you had an aunt who was in charge of Children's Hour? Who cared if you had a pen friend in Canada who had sent you a dollar and a dried maple leaf? Or if you had a cousin who was given a pound note for her birthday? So you had a tea set, a dolls' house! You had new shoes, a diamond clasp in your hair, a new velvet hair ribbon! You were going for a holiday to the North Island, on the boat!

But had you walked across the pipe?

The din of rumor in the whole world, knocking against the sky, and the patent-leather sun shining and the shredded hawthorn turning brown in drifts in the gutters, and the rain raining forty days and forty nights, and the town clock chiming, the echoing and gonging of boastings and braveries were too much, too much to bear. They lasted for years of anguish. Each morning when we woke and were let loose in the placid area of neat thinking and ordinary values like being best at sums, being allowed to stay up late, having a season ticket to the baths, being an heiress an orphan or a changeling, we found that thoughts of the pipe had jumped the queue and sneaked in before everything else, upsetting all the neatness. Who would walk the pipe today? that was the question. There seemed to be nothing left for

45

me but wishing. I linked little fingers with people and wished.

The first of the month came. I said Rabbits, and wished again. Rumors and longings spurted like fountains into the sky.

I never walked across the pipe.

Mercifully, fashions change. So many people in the street seemed suddenly to be getting married, and there were tin-cannings to arrange, and rivalry as to who would be given the most to eat. Someone made history by riding a bicycle down Glenn Street with no hands. The empty house, which belonged to us by right and in which we played day after day, was suddenly occupied, with curtains in the windows, and a fierce man standing at the door and shouting to us, "Hop-It-You." Someone found out that the juice of the creeper growing along the bank would cure warts, that if you sucked the stem of the purple clover and said the alphabet backward you would know who you were going to marry.

And a new big store was opening downtown in the main street. It was called the Self-Help, and what could that mean but that you could go in and help yourself whenever you wanted to?

So many things to do, so many claims to stake. The pipe was almost forgotten.

And now, today, I remember it once more. We are no longer the brave and the cowardly. But the division is there, it is frightening, we dare not investigate it. We are merely trying to ignore the notice DANGER, ANGER, and, with or without witnesses, to cross, the hard way, the unfathomable darkness between man and man.

stink-pot

Someone began to call my sister Stink-pot. Soon all the children at school were calling her Stink-pot with the result that, gumming events together and tying possibilities like the tails of paper kites, they began to call out to me, all along Reed Street and Ribble Street and down Dee Street where Beverly Willis lived who had been to Australia. "You're Stink-pot Wellaby's sister."

To tell the truth our name was not Wellaby but one of my secret longings was to have a name with three syllables, therefore I have named us Wellaby.

"You're Stink-pot Wellaby's sister!"

See how distinguished it looks and sounds. But all the same it was an insult.

At first I was indignant and defended the rights of my family by retaliating with a feeble "She's not a Stink-pot."

Then, growing cunning, for affairs were not as peaceful as they should have been between Molly and me, I introduced her new label into our home, to protect myself against bullying or sly elder-sister maneuvers.

"Stink-pot," I said.

"Mum, Nini's called me Stink-pot!"

From the kitchen came my mother's voice answering, "Don't quarrel, kiddies. Love one another. Say nice words to each other!"

How I hated my mother! There was never any variation in her advice, it was always, Love one another, and at night when darkness threatened it was always, Think about nice things, about sunshine and fairies.

Sunshine and fairies! I never knew fairies, and if I did I would not have cared to invite them to my dreams unless they proved themselves capable of engaging in more interesting activities than sitting around on flower petals in ballet dresses, waving wands in the air.

"Stink-pot," I said again to Molly, this time in response to a particularly annoying and painful arm-twist which nearly crippled me.

"Mum, she's called me Stink-pot again!"

This time there was no answer from my mother. She had gone outside to the garden or the clothesline.

Then my sister found a new defense against me.

"All right," she said, with an air of clinching things. She began to chant,

> Sticks and stones will break my bones,
> but names will never hurt me,
> and when I'm dead and in my grave,
> you'll hear the names you called me!

There was something in that rhyme which frightened me, yet I questioned its truthfulness.

"How can I hear the names when you're dead and gone?"

"They'll go over and over in your head. They'll knock at your door lift up the latch walk in; all the names you've ever called me in your life from when you were the size of a flea."

"I never was the size of a flea!"

"That's all *you* know about it. You were the size of a peanut, a monkeynut, same thing ha ha, and a grape and a spider and a flea and an earwig with a copper overcoat."

"I never was. I don't often call you names, anyway."

"You do. What about S-T-I-N-K [she was spelling it out] P-O-T?"

I grew daring. "Stink-pot, Stink-pot!" I cried.

"You'll see," Molly said. "You'll see when I'm dead and gone and in my grave."

And she twisted my arm once more, and caught at my wrist, giving me a vicious Chinese and Maori burn combined.

There was no precedent. Molly died. And not long after her death I was lying in bed one night waiting for the names to come after me. If they're going to haunt me, and I'm going to hear them, it will be now, I thought. It will be tonight. I waited.

Sticks and stones will break my bones,
but names will never hurt me,
and when I'm dead and in my grave
you'll hear the names you called me.

I listened hard, considering the possibilities. Molly was dead and in her grave; the requirements of the verse were complete. I had said "No" when my mother asked, "Do you want to look at Molly before she is buried?" I was wishing now that I hadn't said "No." But she had been lying in the room amongst the smell of sturmer apples, and that had seemed strange. I supposed that at that very moment she was sending out the lists of names as quickly as she could, wasting no time, now that she was dead and in her grave. Besides Stink-pot I remembered Knock-knees, Pick-the-Pie, loony, greedy-guts, Fatty Arbuckle, Bandy-legs, not to mention the names of all the boys she had been sweet on, starting from Harry Hunt and ending up with Ted Hamilton.

I was lonely in the big bed that night. I unscrewed one of the knobs at the foot of the bed and picked out the piece of paper with the code message that we had posted to each other weeks ago. Alas, it was so long ago that we had played that game, I couldn't understand the message, I had forgotten the code.

I tore up the message.

Then I lay down again, waiting for the names. When I'm dead and in my grave you'll hear the names you called me. I knew that if I were going to hear them at all it would be that night, for Molly had been dead long enough to have arranged everything, every kind of revenge and torture. I knew for certain that if the names came it would be then, as I lay alone in the big bed, listening to the owls in the trees, and the small birds calling suddenly, startled from their sleep in the hedge.

I listened so hard, holding my breath in case I blew away the sound. I had gathered from Molly's chanting that when I did hear the names the experience would be very unpleasant, and perhaps would even drive me, in my turn, to the grave.

50

I wondered if Molly were feeling cold, if she were hungry or thirsty, if she remembered the code message hidden in the bed-knob and could translate the code.

And all the time I was listening for the names. I listened so hard, all night until the early morning. And I heard no names, not one name, not even Stink-pot.

In the end I turned over to go to sleep. I always knew Molly was a liar.

"Liar, liar!" I whispered triumphantly into my pillow.

"Hecate, you look angerly"

It was always Molly Cochrane who was chosen to read the best parts, though her voice, having been through a juice extractor, was shredded dry, with little substance; it also seemed to ride switchback in the air. It was not, I thought, the kind of voice for reading poems or the best parts in plays. Nevertheless Molly Cochrane was always chosen.

She was the most popular girl in the class, and popularity mattered, and was gauged at the beginning of each year by our voting for a Sports Captain and a Form Captain which honors were given, year after year, to Brenda Langley and Molly Cochrane who were close friends and the center attraction of the Form Five, the leaders of the class in everything except studies—and who cared about studies?

Molly Cochrane played the piano for us to march in and out of Assembly in the mornings; she played the hymns, and many of the songs in the music class, "Lonely Woods with Paths Dim and Silent," "A Haunt of Peace for Weary-hearted," and "The Glow of Evening Tints the Bay Where Cloudlets Kiss the Sea."

Molly Cochrane had so many advantages. Her father was the Town Mayor and one of the Governors of the School Board. Her mother was Chairwoman of the Ladies' Guild. Molly was honest, kind; she had all the virtues, and a talent for everything except studies, and even there she had her moments of shining; she won the Isabel Smith Memorial Essay: title: "Pleasure from Work."

Isabel Smith, a nurse, had died in a hospital ship which had been torpedoed during the First World War. I remember my own long rambling essay in which I described Isabel Smith, dressed in white, appearing from the depths of the sea and crying, Pleasure from Work, Pleasure from Work; in that way, I felt, I would be appeasing those who were responsible for the dull title (and who incidentally would decide the winner), and the memory of the woman who had given her name to the essay. But my ruse did not work. There was some confusion. I dressed Isabel Smith in white marquisette, surely an appropriate material for a ghost; but the name of her ship had been the "Marquette," and the ghostly cries Pleasure from Work Pleasure from Work along with innumerable "Marquettes" and marquisettes must have made my essay an object of ridicule.

But who, except Molly Cochrane, could have won the prize?

She lunched at school with Brenda Langley and the three other girls who ruled the form fashions, opinions, predictions. The five were always together; they always had something to say, not mere remarks, but interesting tales of weekend expeditions, holidays, picnics at the beach. Their lives seemed to possess an abundance of excitement and laughter. Their enjoyment of their home life, of the members of their family, their leisure, their school hours, seemed on a scale apart.

I kept dumb about my home life. I could not spend half an hour describing what my little brother said at breakfast (if I'd had a little brother), and make it sound such an exciting experience that the lack of it would arouse envy in others and lessen their measure of happiness. As the five sat lunching on the seat outside the Common Room or in summer on the lawn by the tennis courts, and their laughter burst from them, and their voices sounded, full of enjoyment and interest, their lives seemed near perfection. They lacked nothing—at least not love or money or the prospect of tomorrow; they were completely safe.

How I envied them! Everything they talked of seemed to contain a special significance and pleasure.

During the lunch hour I sat with Rona Todd, just Rona Todd, who was a bore, and told me about her arm which had been in plaster for months, and about the specialist in Dunedin who was so high up in his profession that he was called Mister instead of Doctor. She also talked on and on about her wonderful brothers. If the same conversation had come from the lips of the Five it would have been charged with importance and fascination. From Rona, it was boring. I was tired of her arm and her specialist and her brothers. Nevertheless we lunched together and achieved the unity of not being one of the Five. My lunch had the butter skimped on it, and the tomatoes were crushed and bleeding through the wet bread, while the cakes which my mother had baked with such care the evening before, and which had seemed so appetizing and golden against the black oven tray, had suffered a strange distortion in their journey from home to school, and appeared now as haphazard shapes scarred with burns and outcrops of pale dough.

Who had changed them, between the time I put them in the brown paper bag and my case and the time I unwrapped them to eat while Rona Todd sat beside me talking about her arm, her specialist, her wonderful brothers? There was a deception somewhere; I could not understand it.

Nor could I understand how my home and family changed as soon as I arrived at school each day. My mother had sent her measurements up to Horsham's, the Mail-Order Firm in Christchurch, and for the first time for years my mother was to have a new dress, made of silk, real silk, with a matching coat, and a new hat if there was enough money left. At home, the news had seemed worth talking about; at school, it was no news at all. My pride in the new dress turned to shame. I realized that my mother's voice was high-pitched, in a permanent state of panic, that her clothes were shabby, that she had to send to a Mail-Order Firm because no clothes in the shops would fit her, she was so big; that she never went visiting or belonged to Guilds, like Molly Cochrane's mother, or presided over Sales of Work; that she never came to school on Parents' Day or to the Garden Party at the end of the year when we wore our white dresses, played Maori stick games, sang "Now is the Month of Maying" and "Go Lovely Rose," and sold pot holders, baskets, coconut ice.

On the other hand, the parents of the Five . . .

Oh dear, I did not even have a serviette to spread my lunch upon! Everyone, including Rona Todd and greasy-haired Eileen Walls who cheated at geography, had a serviette at lunchtime, while my own lunch-covering was warped brown paper with advertisements for tea written on the outside in bold blue letters.

Life was indeed bitterly unsatisfying.

Especially as Molly Cochrane always had the best parts in the plays and the poems. The teacher would ask (knowing well the answer), "Now who shall we ask to read this. Ah, Molly, will you read it for us?"

I was not the only one to suffer. I knew one girl who longed to read a part in a play, yet during her entire school days the only words she uttered from the stage were (as eldest son in a quick entrance and exit), "Give *me* the letter!"

I remember also another girl whose one line read, "They have their dreams and do not think of us."

With Molly Cochrane always in the best part, and the other parts distributed among the powerful Four and one or two girls on the fringe of power, the remainder of the class, including myself, had to be satisfied with being Cobweb, Moth, Mustard Seed, or Courtiers, First, Second or Third Soldier, uttering monosyllables or short sentences: "Here." "Ready." "No." "The army advances." "The King is here"—with the King striding in to greet his Queen (Molly Cochrane, of course), who delivered half a page or indeed a whole page of speech while we murmured our occasional, "My Lord. Avaunt Thee. Away Your Majesty."

There is no need for me to reveal who played the parts of Portia, Ophelia, Desdemona, Hermia, Mark Antony. . . .

And then, suddenly, the situation changed. Miss Dawson arrived back from overseas. We had never been taught by Miss Dawson who was a slight dark woman with a flushed turnipy face, soft blue eyes, and an ugly body; her gown seemed to conceal a deformity which we never defined, in spite of rumor and speculation. Upon taking over our class she immediately seized upon tiny wizened Joan Ward as her favorite pupil; the two resembled each other. When Miss

Dawson talked of people and their stature she would put in a kindly word for the undersized.

"Like Joan and me," she would say, laughing, and adding, "Like Alexander Pope, Napoleon . . ."

It is wonderful how people can dissect the famous, removing fragments of them to fit, like pieces of a jigsaw puzzle, into their own lives.

In explanation for Miss Dawson's spinsterhood we did not give (as with other teachers) the tale of "her boy was killed in the war," because we had an idea that nobody had ever asked Miss Dawson to marry. She lived with her mother and an Airedale dog in a small house with smoking chimneys and a pointed roof made of confectionery. When she came to teach us her talk was full of the great event of her life—her journey overseas—and many an afternoon we suffered while the room was darkened with drawn blinds, a sheet screen was hung in front of the desks, and Miss Dawson, controlling the old-fashioned projector at the back of the room, showed us lantern slides of the British Isles. We gazed, bored, at the trapped trophies of her journey—postcard pictures of Dove Cottage, Haworth Parsonage, Tintern Abbey, while Miss Dawson talked on and on of her experiences which would have been interesting had they been related apart, in daylight, but which combined with the darkness and with our inward rebellion against all types of lantern slides (our only type had been photos of Bible Lands shown to us by missionaries) produced a soporific daze in us. Yet we gave Miss Dawson no trouble by misbehaving. We were sympathetic to her. We realized that her journey overseas had been such a tremendous experience that she could not be expected to keep it entirely to herself, her mother, her Airedale dog and Miss Lorimer, the commercial teacher who had traveled with her.

"The day we went to Stratford on Avon . . ."
"The journey to Stonehenge where we . . ."
"London—ah London!"
Sometimes we wondered what would be in store for us
when the phase of lantern slides had passed.
We soon found out. Our play for that term was to be
Macbeth, and so far no mention had been made of it. When
we entered the classroom one morning, Miss Dawson turned
upon us, and twisting her already ugly face with an evil
witch-like expression she quavered in sinister tones,

> When shall we three meet again,
> In thunder, lightning or in rain?

It was Macbeth arrived in the classroom.

The day came when we were to read the play in front of
the class—that curious anonymity of struggling scholars
who were good at games and stupid at mathematics or clever
at both, whose understanding could be penetrated in French
but not in Science, who played the role of spectators in the
gymnasium, or leapt about in rompers and blouse, executing
perfect forward or backward rolls; whose fathers were or
were not on the School Board, who were rich or poor; girls
who blossomed and had affairs with the High School Boys;
girls who cheated, were shifty-eyed, pimply-faced, buxom,
pretty, plain, scatty, studious, tall, thin. . . .

I was not particularly interested in the choice of parts that
day. I knew there was always Molly Cochrane, and not even
Miss Dawson had been able to resist her spell. In one week
Molly Cochrane had been asked to read lines from "The
Scholar Gipsy," "Dover Beach," "The Grammarian's Funeral"—"Here, here's his place where meteors shoot, stars
form, lightnings are loosened."

I had given up hope of ever saying much beyond "Avaunt

thee" and "He comes, my Lord." Ah, but imagine my surprise and pleasure when Miss Dawson, searching for a suitable Lady Macbeth, looked directly at me—at me, not at Molly Cochrane or Joan Ward or any other!

"I want you to be Lady Macbeth. We will do the sleep-walking scene and learn it and act it in costume at the end of term. We shall also play a scene with the witches. But you are to be Lady Macbeth!"

Then she distributed the rest of the parts including a small one, I think a Third or Second Witch, to Molly Cochrane.

I am still trying to work out the complicated embezzlement of Time. No one ever kept accounts with such a deceptive appearance of honesty.

Again and again I practiced "Out damn spot" before the wardrobe mirror in the front room which was empty except for sturmer apples in winter and coffins when people died.

"Out damn spot, out I say, one, two."

I learned the part thoroughly and waited until the moment arrived when I should act it in front of the class, putting Molly Cochrane and everyone else to shame with my magnificent performance.

But how was I to understand the embezzlement of Time? I have to blame someone. I blame Time who never gave me a chance to walk in my sleep as Lady Macbeth. Time was so preoccupied with School Certificate and examination papers, cisterns, stocks and shares and brokerage, scalene and other triangles, cosines, tangents, logarithms, calculations, measurement of areas, divisions of legacies, Pendlebury's A B and C; and D and E who came late and lost their share in the magical five- and seven-pint vessels . . .

I wanted my share too. I still want it.

I never played Lady Macbeth.

Miss Dawson retired, after having a stroke which left her speech affected. She moved from her confectionery cottage and with her Airedale dog (who, now that Miss Dawson's mother was dead, would sit beside Miss Dawson when she drove her car, looking out of the window, its paws against the glass . . .) she went to live down by the railway station in one of the houses facing the sea. I saw her again only once or twice—driving past in her car (with the dog sitting so confidently in the seat that once belonged to Miss Dawson's mother), and once in the Public Library where the shelves had been made "contemporary," that is, they had been lowered so that one had no privacy when choosing one's book, and was forced to gaze at people's heads and faces over the top of the shelves. I saw Miss Dawson's face over the top of the shelves. ("I want you to be Lady Macbeth.") She was choosing a travel book. Was she planning another journey overseas? Would she return with lantern slides?

Then I remembered that her speech had been affected. They said she could not speak at all, only make signs and gestures, and strange animal noises. She looked more like a witch than ever.

"When shall we three meet again?"

We three? Miss Dawson, Joan Ward, myself?

"I want you to be Lady Macbeth." Was it because Lady Macbeth had red hair? Did Lady Macbeth have red hair? Why did Miss Dawson never keep her promise and let me sleepwalk and wash out my terrible guilt? Shall I write to her now, and ask why?

But now the hypocrite Time even provides his own excuse; it is too late.

All I have is the pleasant memory that I was almost Lady Macbeth, and that Molly Cochrane, Form Captain, leader of the powerful Five, was given a small unimportant part—was it First Witch, Second Witch, Third Witch?—it does not matter. I remember only her one line,

"How now Hecate, you look angerly. . . ."

the bull calf

"Why do I always have to milk the cows?" Olive said. "Couldn't the others do it for a change? But no, it is always me. Up early and over the hills to find Scrapers. At night home from school and over the hills again to find Scrapers, to bring her down across the creek (here it is difficult; I tie a rope over her horns and make my leap first; she follows, if she is willing) through the gate that hangs on one hinge, into the cow byre with its cracked concrete floor. Pinning her in the bail. Putting on the leg rope. Day after day rain shine or snow.

"I'm tired of milking the cows," Olive said. "Beauty, Pansy, and now Scrapers who is bony like bare rafters and scaffolding. One day I will refuse."

Sometimes she did refuse, in the early morning with sleep

gumming her eyes, her body sticky with night, her hair tangled.

"Milk your own cows!" she cried then, retreating to the bedroom and sitting obstinately on the bed, chanting rhymes and French verbs which her mother could not understand because she had left school at sixteen to go to service. . . .

But the thought of Scrapers waiting haunted Olive, and soon she would get up from the bed, clatter to the scullery, bumping into furniture on the way to show her resentment of everything in the world including corners and walls and doors, take the bucket with a swill of warm water in the bottom for washing the teats, and climb the hill in search of Scrapers who, if her bag was full, would be waiting mercifully not far away.

Olive went to High School. In the morning she worried about being late. And every morning when the teacher called suddenly, "Form Twos, Form Twos," Olive worried in case no one formed twos with her. Very often she found herself standing alone. Is it because I stink? she thought. Then she would press the back and front of her uniform, down below, to smooth away the bulge of the homemade sanitary towel, layers of torn sheet sewn together with the blood always leaking through. The other girls used bought towels which were safe and came in packets with tiny blue-edged notices inside the packet, WEAR BLUE LINE AWAY FROM THE BODY. The other girls did not seem to mind when in Drill, which was later called Physical Education to keep up with the times, the teacher would command sharply, "Uniforms Off, Come on Everybody, Uniforms Off!" Why should they mind when they were using towels which did not show, or even the new type where the advertisement had a picture of a woman in a bathing suit, shouting with rapture from the edge of a high-diving board, "No

Belts, No Pins, No Pads!" But on the days when Olive wore her homemade towel she would ask, blushing, "Please can I keep my uniform on?"

"Oh," Miss Copeland said. "Yes."

And Olive and one or two other girls with their uniforms on would huddle miserably on the end seat, by the bar stools, out of everybody's way.

Olive and her sisters had hickies on their chins and foreheads. The advertisements warned them never to wear "off-the-face" hats. Whole pages of the newspapers were devoted to the picture-story of the disasters which befell Lorna, Mary or Marion who continued to wear off-the-face hats in spite of having hickies on their chins and foreheads. Lorna, Mary, Marion were lonely and unwanted until they used Velona Ointment. Olive and her sisters used Velona Ointment. It had a smell like the oil of a motorcar engine and it came off in a sticky grass-green stain on the pillowcase.

But mostly Olive was tired. She stayed up late working mathematical problems, writing French translations and essays, and in the morning she was up so early to go over the hill and find Scrapers. There were so many trees and hollows on the hill, and often it was in these hollows where the grass was juiciest, nourished by the pools of yesterday's rain or the secret underground streams, that Scrapers would be hiding. Sometimes Olive had to walk to the last Reserve before she found Scrapers. Then there was the problem of tying the rope across her horns and leading her home.

Sometimes Scrapers refused to co-operate. Olive would find her dancing up and down, tossing her horns and bellowing.

"Scrapers, Scrapers, come on, be a good cow!"

Still Scrapers refused, Olive could not understand why. I'll be late for school, she thought, after struggling with and trying to chase the entranced cow. But it was no use. Olive would hurry down the hill, across the creek, through the broken-hinged gate and up the path to the house where the family, waiting for breakfast, would ask, "Where's the milk?" while Olive in turn confronted them with her question, "What's the matter with Scrapers? She's dancing and tossing her horns and refusing to be milked."

Her mother received the news calmly. "Leave the cow. She'll be all right in a few days."

Nobody explained. Olive could not understand. She would pour stale milk on her Weet-Bix, finish her breakfast, brush the mud from her shoes, persuade the pleats into her uniform, and hurry away to school.

It was always the same. She stood alone in Assembly, concealing herself behind the girl in front who was taller, Captain of the "A" Basketball Team, Holder of a Drill Shield. Olive did not want the teachers on the platform to see her standing alone, hiding behind the girl in front of her.

Peace perfect peace in this dark world of sin
the cross of Jesus whispers Peace within

she sang, sensing the mystery. Her heart felt heavy and lonely.

When she climbed the hill in search of the cow she always stopped in the paddock next door to pat the neighbor's bull calf which was growing plumper and stronger every day. Everyone knew what happened to bull calves. They were taken to the slaughterhouse while they were still young, or they became steers journeying from saleyard to saleyard until they grew old and tough and despised, without the pride and ferocity of bulls and the gentleness and patience of cows. If you were caught in a paddock with them and they attacked you it was in bursts of irritation which left them standing as if bewildered, half-afraid at their own daring. They did not seem able to decide; they panicked readily; they had no home, they were forever lost in strange surroundings, closed in by new fences and gates with unfamiliar smells, trees, earth; with dogs snapping at their heels, herding them this way and that, in and out, up and down. . . .

Olive knew that one day Ormandy's bull calf would be a steer. "Calfie, calfie," she would whisper, putting her flattened palm inside the calf's mouth and letting it suck.

Night came. The spotted gray cockabullies in the creek wriggled under the stones to sleep, and soon the birds were hushed in the willow trees and the hedge and the sighing pines. This evening Olive was late in fetching Scrapers. She was late and tired. Her best black stockings, cobbled at the back of the leg, were splashed with mud, there were no clean ones for tomorrow; her stockings never lasted, all the other girls bought their stockings at Morton's, and theirs were cashmere, with a purple rim around the top, a sign of quality, while Olive's were made of coarse rayon. She was ashamed of them, she was ashamed of everything and everyone. She kicked her shoes against a clump of grass. Toe and heel plates! Why must she always have toe and heel plates on her shoes? Why must they always be lace-ups? She yawned. Her skin felt itchy. The pressure of her tight uniform upon her breasts was uncomfortable. Why hadn't Aunty Polly realized, and made the seams deeper, to be let out when necessary? Olive's sisters wore uniforms made by real dressmakers. Her sisters were lucky. How they teased her, pointing to the pictures in the True Confession Magazines, digging their elbows slyly at each other and murmuring, "Marylin's breasts were heavy and pendulous."

"That means you," they said to Olive. "You'll be like Mum with two full moons bobbing up and down, moons and balloons and motor tires."

Yes, her sisters were lucky.

"Why don't they help with the cow?" Olive asked. "Why don't they milk the cow for a change?"

She walked slowly up the hill, keeping to the path worn by herself and Scrapers; it was rucked with dry, muddy hoofprints and followed along the edge of the pine plantation. When she reached the top of the hill and there was still no sign of Scrapers she went to the fence bordering the native plant reserve and looked out over the town and the sea and the spilled dregs of light draining beyond the horizon. The silver-bellied sea turned and heaved in the slowly brightening moon-track, and the red and green roofs of the town were brushed with rising mist and moon. She identified objects and places: the Town Clock; the main street; the houseboat down at the wharf; the High School, and just behind the trees at the corner, next to the bicycle sheds, the little shop that sold hot mince pies and fish and chips at lunchtime. Then she gazed once more at the sea, waiting for the Sea-Foam-Youth-Grown-Old to appear. It was her secret dream. She knew he would never reach her. She knew that his bright glistening body became old, shriveled, yellow, as soon as he touched the sand; it was the penalty. She sighed. The grieving hush-hush of the trees disturbed her. Their heads were bowed, banded with night. The wind moved among them, sighing, only increasing their sorrow. It came to her, too, with its moaning that she could not understand; it filled the world with its loneliness and darkness.

Olive sighed again. What was the use of waiting for the Sea-Foam-Youth-Grown-Old? What was the use of anything? Would the trees never stop saying Why, Why?

She was Olive Blakely going to milk Scrapers. She was Olive Blakely standing on the hill alone at night. The cutty grass and the tinkertailor were brushing against her black stockings; there was bird dirt on the fence post; the barbed wire had snapped and sagged.

That evening she milked Scrapers on the hill. What a miracle! The cow stood motionless for her and did not give those sudden sly kicks which she practiced from time to time. Scrapers was an expert at putting her foot in the bucket.

Olive patted the velvety flank. Scrapers was standing so calmly. Why was she so calm when a few days ago she had danced, tossed, bellowed, jumping fences and running with her tail high in the air? Now she stood peacefully chewing, seeming to count the chews before each swallow, introducing a slight syncopation before returning the cud to her mouth which she opened slowly once or twice in a lazy yawn releasing her warm grassy-smelling breath on the cool air. Her teeth were stained and green, her eyes swam and glistened like goldfish. She let down her milk without protest.

Leaning to one side to balance the full bucket with its froth of creamy milk, Olive walked carefully down the hill. Damn, she thought. I will have to iron my uniform tonight, and sponge it to remove the grass stains. And damn again, I have trodden in cow muck. Cow muck, pancakes, cowpad . . .

She mused on the words. The Welsh children up the road said *cowpad*. They were a compact, aloof, mysterious family with the two girls going to High School. They had a cousin called Myfanwy. Olive wished that she were called Myfanwy. Or Eitne. Or anything except plain pickled Olive.

She crossed the creek. The milk slopped against her legs, dampening her stockings and staining the hem of her uniform.

"Damn again," she said. She would have to look in Pear's *Dictionary*, "Household Hints," to find how to remove milk stains; she never remembered.

Then just as she was approaching the gate she noticed two men leaning over the bull calf in the corner of the paddock, near the hedge. "Mr. Ormandy, Mr. Lewis," Olive said to herself. "Old Ormandy."

He had been named *Old Ormandy* when he stopped people from picking his plums but there was no law against picking them, was there, when the tree hung over the fence into the road, inviting anyone to take the dusty plums split and dark blue with pearls of jelly on their stalk and a bitter, blighted taste at the center, near the stone.

Old Ormandy. The girl Ormandy picked her nose and ate it. Their uncle had been in court for sly-grogging.

Olive watched the two men. What were they doing to the bull calf? It was so dark. What were they doing in the dark? She waited until they had left the bull calf before she went over to say good night to it.

"Calfie, calfie," she whispered. It was lying outstretched. She bent over it, seeking to pat its face and neck. Its nose felt hot and dry, its eyes were bright, and between its back legs there was blood, and a patch of blood on the grass. The calf had been hurt. Old Ormandy and Lewis were responsible. Why hadn't they noticed the calf was ill? Or perhaps they had deliberately been cruel to it?

"I wouldn't put it past them," Olive said aloud, feeling strangely satisfied that she was expressing her indignation in the very words her father used when he became suspicious. "I wouldn't put it past them."

She trembled and patted the calf.

"Calfie, calfie," she whispered again. "Sook sook. Never mind, calfie, I'll get someone to help you."

But her heart was thudding with apprehension. Supposing the calf were to die? She had seen many animals die. They were not pampered and flattered in death, like human beings; they became immediate encumbrances, threats to public health, with neighbors and councilors quarreling over the tedious responsibility of their burial. Or were dead human beings—in secret of course—regarded in this way also, and was their funeral procession a concealment, with flowers, of feelings which the living were afraid to admit? Olive's thoughts frightened her. She knew that all things dead were in the way; you tripped over them, they did not move, they were obstacles, they were no use, even if they were people they were no use, they did not complain or cry out, like sisters, if you pinched them or thumped them on the back, they were simply no use at all.

She did not want the bull calf to die. She could see its eyes glistening, pleading for help. She picked up the milk bucket and hurried through the gate to the house and even before she reached the garden tap (she had to be careful here for the tap leaked, the earth was bogged with moss and onion flower) she heard her father's loud voice talking.

His friends, the Chinese people, had come to visit him, and he was telling the old old story. His operation. He had been ill with appendicitis and while he was in hospital he had made friends with the Chinese family who came often now to visit him, filling the house with unfamiliar voices and excitements, creating an atmosphere that inspired him to add new dimensions of peril to his details of the operation.

"Going gangrene . . . they wheeled me in . . ."

Almost running up to the house, fearing for the life of the bull calf, Olive had time only to hear her father's loud voice talking to the visitors before she opened the kitchen door. She was almost crying now. She was ashamed of her tears in front of the visitors. She tried to calm herself. Everyone looked up, startled.

"It's calfie, Ormandy's bull calf, it's been hurt, there's all blood between its legs and its nose is hot!"

Olive's mother glanced without speaking at her father who returned the glance, with a slight smile at the corner of his mouth. The Chinese visitors stared. One of them, a young man, was holding a bowl with a flower growing in it, a most beautiful water narcissus whose frail white transparent petals made everything else in the room—the cumbersome furniture, the heavy-browed bookcase, the chocolate-colored paneled ceiling, the solid black-leaded stove —seem like unnecessary ballast stored beyond, and at the same time within, people to prevent their lives from springing up joyfully, like the narcissus growing out of water into the clear sky.

"The bull calf, what will we do about it?" Olive urged, breaking the silence, and staring at the flower because she could not take her eyes from its loveliness and frailty.

Her mother spoke. "It's all right," she said. "There's nothing the matter with the calf."

Olive stopped looking at the flower. She turned to her mother. She felt betrayed. Her mother, who took inside the little frozen birds to try to warm them back to life, who mended the rabbit's leg when it was caught in the trap, who fed warm bran to the sick horse that was lying on its side, stretched out!

"But it's bleeding! The calf might die! I saw Mr. Ormandy with it, Old Ormandy and another man!"

She knew the man had been Mr. Lewis, yet she said "another man" because it seemed to convey the terrible anonymity which had suddenly spread over every person and every deed. Nobody was responsible; nobody would own up; nobody would even *say*.

"The bull calf's all right, I tell you," her father said, impatient to return to his story of the operation. "Forget it. Go and do your homework."

Olive sensed embarrassment. They seemed ashamed of her. They were ashamed of something. Why didn't they tell? She wished she had not mentioned the bull calf.

"But I saw it with my own eyes," she insisted, in final proof that the calf was hurt and needed help.

Again everybody was silent. She could not understand. Why were they so secretive? What was the mystery?

Then her father swiftly changed the subject.

"Yes, they wheeled me in . . . going gangrene . . . I said to Lottie, I said, on the night . . . ."

Olive was about to go from the room when the young man in the corner beckoned to her. He smiled. He seemed to understand. He held out the bowl with the narcissus in it, and said, "You have it. It is for you."

Gratefully she took the bowl, and making no further mention of the sick calf she went to her bedroom. She put the narcissus on her dressing table. She touched the petals gently, stroking them, marveling again at the transparency of the whole flower and the clear water where every fiber of the bulb seemed visible and in motion as if brushed by secret currents and tides. She leaned suddenly and put her cheek against the flower.

Then she lay down on her bed and with her face pressed to the pillow, she began to cry.

the teacup

When he came to live in the same house she hoped that he would be friendlier, take a deeper interest in her, invite her to the pictures or to go dancing with him or in the summer walking arm in arm in the park. They might even go for a day to the seaside, she thought, or on one of those bus tours visiting Windsor Castle, London Airport, or the Kentish Hopfields. How exciting it would be!

He had been working at the factory for over two years now, since he came out of the Army, and they had often spoken to each other during the day, shared football coupons and bets in the Grand National, lunched together at the staff canteen where you could get a decent meal for two and ten, extra for tea, coffee, and bread and butter. He had talked to her of his family, how they were all dead except his brother and himself; of his life in the Army, traveling the world, a good life, India, Japan, Germany. Once or twice he had mentioned (this was certain and had made her heart flurry) that he would like to "find someone and settle down."

He needs someone, she thought. He is quite alone and needs someone.

She told him of her own life, how she had thought of emigrating to Australia and had gone to Australia House where an official asked her age and when she told him he said sharply, "We are looking for younger people; the young and the skilled."

She was forty-four. They did not want people of forty-four in Australia. Not single women.

"They wouldn't take me either," he had said, and, quick with sympathy she had exclaimed, "Oh, Bill!"

She had never called him by his first name before. He had always been Mr. Forest. He addressed her as Miss Rogers, but she knew that if they became closer friends he would call her Edith, that is, Edie. She told him that she was staying in South London, living in a room in a house belonging to this family; that she knitted jerseys for the little girl, helped the landlady with the washing and sewing, and looked after the bird and the cat when the family went on holiday. She told how regularly every second weekend she stayed with her sister at Blackheath, for a change; how her other sister had emigrated years ago to Australia and now was married with three children and a house of her own, she sent photos of the family, you could see them outside in the garden in the sun and how brown the children looked and the garden was bright with flowers, tropical blooms that you never see in England except in Kew Gardens, and wasn't it hot there under glass among the rubber plants? But the photos never showed her sister's husband, for they were separated, he had left her; her other sister's husband had gone too, packed up and vanished, even while his daughter still suffered from back trouble and now she was grown up and crippled, lying on the sofa all day, but managing wonderfully with the district nurse coming on Wednesday afternoons, no, Tuesdays, Wednesday was early closing. And her sister's son had a grant to study accountancy, he would qualify, there was a future ahead of him. . . .

So they talked together, and soon it was commonplace for him to call her Edith (not Edie, not yet) and her to say Bill, though in front of the others at work they still said Miss Rogers and Mr. Forest. Then one night she invited him home for tea, and he accepted the invitation. How happy she was that evening! How she wished it had been her own home with her own furniture and curtains and not just one room and the small shared kitchen but two or three or four rooms to walk in and out of, opening and closing the doors, each room serving its purpose, one for visitors, another . . .

She bought extra food that evening, far too much, and it turned out that he didn't care for what she had bought, and he didn't mind saying so, politely of course, but he had been in the Army and was used to speaking his mind.

"There's no fuss in the Army. You say what you think."

"Of course it's best," she said, trying not to sound disappointed because he did not care for golden sponge pudding and had preferred not to sample the peeled shrimps, cocktail brand.

But on the whole they spent a pleasant evening. She knitted, and showed him photographs of her family. They went for a short walk in the park and while they were walking she linked her arm with his, as she had seen other women do, and her eyes were bright with happiness. She mentioned to him that a small room was vacant on the top floor where she stayed, and that if ever he decided to change his lodging wouldn't it be a good idea if he took the room?

She could manage things for him; she could arrange meals, see to shopping and washing; he would be independent of course. . . .

A few weeks later when he had been on holiday at his brother's and had arrived back at his lodgings only to find that the two women of the house, having decided after waiting long enough that he was definitely not going to ask one of them to marry him, had given him notice to leave, he remembered the vacancy that Miss Rogers— Edith—had mentioned, and one week later he had come to live in the house, half a flight of stairs up from her own room.

She helped to prepare his room. She cleaned the windows and drew the curtains wide to give him full advantage of the view—the back gardens of the two or three adjacent houses, the road beyond, with the Pink Paraffin lorries parked outside their store; the garden of the large house belonging to the County Councilor.

She made the bed, draping the candlewick bedspread, shelving it at the top beneath the pillows, shifting the small table from the corner near the door to a more convenient position near the head of the bed.

A reading lamp? Would he need a reading lamp?

With a tremble of excitement she realized that she knew nothing about him, that from now on, each day would be filled to the brim with discovery. Either he read in bed or he didn't read in bed. Did he like a cup of tea in the early morning? What did he do in the evenings? What did he sound like when he coughed in the middle of the night when all was quiet?

Downstairs in the small kitchen which she shared with

Jean, another lodger in the house, an unmarried woman a few years younger than herself, she segregated on a special shelf covered by half a yard of green plastic which hung, scalloped at the edge, the utensils he would need for his meals; his own special spoon, knife, fork. On the top shelf there were two large cups, one with the handle broken. Jean had broken it. She had confessed long ago but the subject still came up between her and Edith and always served to discharge irritation between them.

As Edith was choosing the special teacup to be used solely by Bill, she picked up the handleless one, and remarked to Jean, "These are nice cups, they hold plenty of tea, but that woman from Australia who used to stay in the room before you came, she broke the handle off this cup."

"No, I broke it," Jean confessed again.

"No. It was that woman from Australia who stayed here in the room before you came. I was going to emigrate to Australia once. I went as far as getting the papers and filling them in."

The woman from Australia had also been responsible for other breakages and inconveniences. She had never cleaned the gas stove, she had blocked the sink with vegetables, she hadn't fitted in with arrangements for bathing and washing, and the steam from her baths had peeled the wallpaper off the bathroom wall, newly decorated too. She had left behind a miscellany of objects which were labeled as "belonging to the woman from Australia" and which Edith carefully preserved and replaced when the cupboards were cleaned out, as if the woman from Australia were still a needful presence in the house.

Attached to the special shelf prepared for Bill there was a row of golden cuphooks; upon one of them Edith hung the teacup she had chosen for him, a large deep cup with a gold, green and dark-blue pattern around the rim and the words ARKLOW POTTERY EIRE DONEGAL, encircled by a smudged blue capital *E*, printed underneath. In every way the teacup seemed specially right for Bill. How Edith longed for him to be settled in, having his tea, with her pouring from the new teapot warmed under its new cozy, into his special teacup!

He took two heaped spoons of sugar, she shivered with excitement at remembering.

On Bill's first night she could not disguise her happiness. They left work together that night, they came home sitting side by side on the top deck of the bus, they walked together from the bus stop down and along the road to the house. His luggage had already been delivered; it stood in the corridor, strapped and bulging, mysterious, exciting, with foreign labels.

And now there was the bliss of showing him his room, the ins and outs of his new lodgings—the bathroom, telling him on which day he could bathe, showing him how to turn on the hot water,

"Up is on, Down is off. . . ."

Explaining, pointing out, revealing, with her cheeks flushed and her breast rising and falling quickly to get enough breath for speech because the details, all the pointing out and revealing were fraught with so much excitement.

At last she led him to the cupboard in the kitchen.

"This is your shelf. Here is your knife, fork, spoon. Of course you can always take anything, anything you want from my shelf, here, this one here, but not from Jean's."

"Anything you want," she said again, urgently, "take from my shelf, won't you?"

Then she paused.

"And this is your special cup and saucer."

She detached the cup from its golden hook and held it to the light. He looked approvingly at it.

"Nice and big," he said.

She glowed.

"That's why I chose it from the others. There used to be two of them, but that woman from Australia who stayed here broke the handle of one."

She still held the teacup as if she were reluctant to return it to its place on the hook.

"Isn't it roomy?" she said, seeking, in a way, for further acknowledgment from him.

But he had turned his attention elsewhere. He was hungry. He sniffed at the food already cooking.

They had dinner then. She had prepared everything—the stewed beef, potatoes, carrots, onions, cabbage. His place was laid at the small table which was really a cabinet and was therefore awkward to sit at, as one's knees bumped into its cupboard door. She apologized for the table, and thought, I'll have to look around for a cheap table, perhaps one with a formica top, easily cleaned, Oh dear there is so much furniture we need, and those lace curtains need renewing, just from where I am sitting I can see they are almost in shreds.

And she sighed with the happy responsibility of everything.

After dinner she washed the dishes, showed him where to hang his bath towel, and where to put his shaving gear, before he went upstairs to lie on his bed and read the evening paper. Then, sharp at half-past eight, she put the kettle on (she hadn't noticed before how furred it was, and dented at the sides, she would have to see about a new kettle) and when the water was boiling she made two cups of tea, taking one up to his room and knocking gently on the door.

"Can I come in, Bill?"

"Yes, come in."

He was rather irritated at being interrupted, and showed his irritation by frowning at her, for he had of course been in the Army and he believed in directness, in speaking out.

She stood a moment, timidly, in the doorway.

"I've brought you a cup of tea."

She handed him his special teacup on its matching saucer.

"That's good of you."

He took it, and blew the parcels from the top. She stayed a while, talking, while he drank his tea. She asked him how he liked his new lodging. She told him there were a few shops around the corner, two cinemas further down the road "showing nice programs of an evening," and that in summer the park nearby was lovely to sit and walk in.

Then he told her that he was tired, all this changing around, that he was going to bed to get some sleep.

"See you in the morning," she said.

She took the cups and went downstairs to the kitchen to tidy up for the night. Jean was in the kitchen filling her hot-water bottle. Edith glanced at her, not being able to conceal her joy. Jean had no friend to stay, she had no one to cook for, to wash for. Edith began to talk of Bill.

"I'll be up earlier than usual tomorrow," she said. "There's Bill's breakfast to get. He has two boiled eggs every morning," she said, pausing for Jean to express the wonder which should be aroused at the thought of two boiled eggs for breakfast.

"Does he?" Jean exclaimed, faintly admiring, envious.

"I'm calling him in the morning as he finds it difficult to wake up. Some men do, you know."

"Yes," Jean said. "I know."

Early next morning Edith was bustling about the kitchen attending to Bill and his toilet and breakfast needs—putting on hot water for the shave, boiling the two eggs, and then sharp at twenty to eight they set out together to catch the bus for work, walking up the road arm in arm. Bill wore a navy-blue duffle coat and carried a canvas bag. The morning light caught the sandy color of his thinning hair, and showed the pink baldness near his temples and the pink confectionery tint of his cheeks. She was wearing her heavy brown tweed coat and the fawn flowerpot hat which she had bought when her sister took her shopping at Blackheath. Clothes were cheaper yet more attractive in Blackheath; the market was full of bargains—why was it not so, Edith wondered, in her home territory, why did other people always live where really good things were marked down, going for a song, though the flowerpot hat was not cheap. Edith had long ago given up worrying over the hat. She had felt uneasy about it—perhaps it would go suddenly out of fashion, and although she never kept consciously in fashion, whenever there was a topsy-turvy revolution with waists going up or down and busts being annihilated, Edith had the feeling that the rest of the world had turned a corner and abandoned her. She felt confused, not knowing which track to follow; people were pressing urgently forward, their destinations known and planned, young girls too, half her age. . . .

Edith felt bitter toward the young girls. Why, the tips of their shoes were like hooks or swords, anyone could see they were a danger.

But everything was different now: there was Bill.

Each night they walked home, again arm in arm, separating at the shops where Edith bought supplies for their dinner while Bill went on to the house, put his bag away, had a wash, and sat cozily on a chair in the kitchen, reading the evening paper and waiting for his dinner to be prepared. They had dinner, sitting awkwardly at the table-cabinet, with Edith each night apologizing, remarking that one weekend she would scout around at Blackheath for a cheap table.

"The wallpaper wants doing, too," she said one evening, looking thoughtfully at the torn paper over the fireplace. To her joy Bill took the hint.

"I'm not bad at decorating," he said. "Being in the Army, you know."

She laughed impatiently and blushed.

"But you're not in the Army now, you're settling down!"

He agreed. "Yes, it's time I settled down."

He spent the following weekend papering the kitchen, and although it was Edith's usual time for visiting her sister, she did not go to Blackheath but stayed in the kitchen, making cups of tea for Bill, fetching, carrying, admiring, talking to him, holding equipment for him, and by Sunday evening when the job was finished and the kitchen cupboard had been painted too, and the window sills, and even new curtains hung on plastic hooks which were rustproof and could be washed free of dust and soot, the two sat together, in deep contentment, drinking their cups of tea and eating their slices of white bread and apricot jam, homemade.

But Edith's satisfaction was chilled by the persistent thought, It isn't even my own home, it isn't even my own home. Still, she consoled herself, in time, who knows?

Their routine was established. Every evening it was the same—dinner, apologies over the awkward shape of the table (but why, she thought, should I spend money on a table when it isn't even my own home?), meager conversation, a

few exclamations, statements, revival of rumors; the newspapers to read. . . . They each bought their own evening
paper, and after they both had finished reading they exchanged papers, with a dreamlike movement, for they were
at the same time concentrating on their stewed beef or fried
chops or fish.

"There's the same news in both, really."

"Yes, there's not much difference."

Nevertheless they exchanged papers and settled once
more to eat and read. When they had finished she would say,
"I'll do the dishes."

At first Bill used to walk around with a tea towel hanging
over his arm. Later, when he realized that his help was not
needed, he didn't bother to remove the towel from the
railing behind the kitchen door. There were three railings,
one each for Edith, Jean, and Bill. Edith had bought Bill a
special tea towel, red and blue (colorfast) with a matador
and two bulls printed on it.

One evening when Edith was not feeling tired she said she
would like to go to the pictures, that there was a good one
showing down the road, and if they hurried they would get
in at the beginning of the main picture, or halfway through
Look at Life.

Bill was not interested.

"Not for me, not tonight."

He went upstairs to make the final preparations and judg-
ments for the filling-in of the football coupon, while Edith
retired to her room, switched on the electric fire, and sat in
her armchair, knitting. The glow from the fire sent bars of
light, like burns, across her face. Her eyes watered a little
as she leaned forward to follow the pattern. The wool felt
thick and rough against her fingers.

I must be tired after all, she thought, and put down her knitting.

At half-past eight she went to the kitchen to make the usual cup of tea, and as she said good night to Bill she thought, He's tired after that heavy packing at work all day. Maybe in the weekends we'll go out together somewhere, to the pictures or the park.

The next morning when it was time to set out for work it seemed that Bill was not quite ready, there were a few things to see to, he said. So Edith went alone up the road to the bus stop, and later Bill set out for work alone. And that night they came home separately. And after that, every morning and evening they went to and from work alone.

In the weekend Bill mentioned that he knew friends who kept a pub in Covent Garden, that he would be spending the weekend there. Soon he spent every weekend there. At night he still came home for meals, but sometimes he neglected to say that he wasn't coming home, and Edith would make elaborate preparations for dinner, only to find that she had to eat it alone.

"If only he would tell me," she complained to Jean. "I see him at work during the day, and for some reason he's even ashamed to let on that he stays here. Afraid the others will tease him."

She smiled wistfully, a little secretively, as if perhaps there might be cause for teasing.

Well, she thought, at least he sleeps here.

And was there not all the satisfying flurry in the morning of heating his shaving-water, putting the two eggs to boil, leaving the kettle on low gas in case he needed it, setting his place at the table with his plate, his knife, and, carefully at the side, his special teacup and saucer? And then taking possession of details concerning him, as if they were property being signed to her alone? He eats far too much salt. One drum of salt lasts no time with him. How can he eat so much black pudding? He's fond of sugar, too.

He likes, he prefers, he would rather have . . .

He'd be lost without his cup of tea.

Yes, that was one thing he was always ready for, she could always make him a cup of tea.

And then there were his personal habits which she treasured as legacies, as if his gradual withdrawal from her had been concerned, in a way, with death, wills and next-of-kin, with her being the sole beneficiary.

"Why, oh why, does he leave all his pairs of socks to be washed at once?"—said in a voice at the same time complaining and proud—"I've told him to bring his dirty clothing down for me to wash, but he persists in leaving it in his room, and there I have to go and search about in his most private clothing, and I never know where he keeps anything!"—said in a voice warm with satisfaction.

It was true that her washing seemed endless, and lasted all Saturday morning, and the ironing took all Sunday morning or Monday evening. She liked ironing his shirts, underclothes and handkerchiefs. She tried to accept the fact that he was not inclined to take her out anywhere, not even to the pictures or the park, that he did not care to accompany her to or from work. Once or twice she reminded him that he was getting old, that he was forty-seven, that she was about the same age . . . perhaps they could spend the rest of their lives together, life was not all dizzy romance, perhaps they could marry . . . she would look after him, see to him. . . .

"But I like my freedom," he said.

Then she tried to frighten him into thoughts of himself as a lonely old man with no one to care for him and no one to talk to.

"If it happens," he said, "it happens. I've been in the Army, you know, around in Japan, India, Germany, I've seen a thing or two."

As if being in the Army had provided him with special defenses and privileges. And it had, hadn't it? He could speak his mind, he knew what he was up to. . . .

So the wonderful hopes which had filled Edith's mind when Bill had first come to stay, began to fade. Why won't he see? she thought. I'm trying to do my best for him. It would be nice, in summer, to walk arm in arm in the park.

Meanwhile her stated attitude became, I don't care, it doesn't worry me.

The Council were starting a course of dancing lessons for beginners over thirty. She began to go dancing in the evenings, and when she came home she would tell Jean about the lovely time she had enjoyed.

"I go with the girl from work. Her father has that gray Jaguar with the toy leopard in the back."

"You want to go dancing," she suggested one night to Jean.

"Oh," Jean replied. "I had a friend to visit me."

"A friend? A man?"

"Yes. A man."

"I didn't see him."

"Oh, he came to visit me."

Sometimes Edith went dancing twice a week now, and Bill came home or didn't come home to dinner. Still, rather wistfully, Edith prepared food for him, peeled the potatoes (he was fond of potatoes), cleaned the Brussels sprouts, or left little notes with directions in them: "The sausages from yesterday are in the oven if you care for them. There's soup in the enamel jug. There are half a dozen best eggs on my shelf . . . or if you fancy baked beans . . ."

Edith noticed that Jean's new friend seemed to bring her a plentiful supply of food. Why, sometimes her shelf was filled to overflowing. She hoped that Bill had remembered not to touch anything upon Jean's shelf.

"My friend's good that way," Jean said. "And he always lets me know when he is coming to visit me."

Edith flushed.

"Bill would let me know about dinner and suchlike, but I don't see him much during the day, not now he's working upstairs. He's very thoughtful underneath, Bill is."

"My friend bought me underwear for Christmas. Do you think I should have accepted it?"

"It's rather personal isn't it?"

Bill had not given Edith a present.

"Oh there's nothing between us," Jean assured her.

"Bill wanted to give me something but I wouldn't have it. I said I enjoy what I'm doing for him and that's that. You say your friend came on Saturday? I've never seen him yet."

"You always miss him, don't you?"

That was Monday.

That night when Bill had come home, eaten his dinner, and gone to his room, and Edith had put the kettle on the gas and was setting out the cups for tea, she noticed that Bill's cup was missing, the big teacup with the gold, dark-blue and light-green decorations and the words printed at the bottom, the big teacup, Bill's cup, that hung always on the golden hook.

With a feeling of panic she searched Bill's shelf, Jean's, her own, and the cupboards underneath, removing the grater and flour sifter, the cake tins, and the two battered saucepans which had belonged to the woman from Australia.

She could not find the teacup.

She hurried from the kitchen and up to Bill's room.

"Bill," she called, "your cup's missing!"

A sleepy voice sounded, "My what?"

She opened the door. He was lying fully dressed on the bed.

He sat up.

Edith's voice was trembling, as if she were bringing him bad news which did not affect him as much as it affected herself, yet which she needed to share.

"Your big teacup that hangs on the hook on your shelf. Have you seen it?"

He spoke abruptly. "No, I haven't seen it."

She looked at him with all the feelings of the past weeks and months working in her face, and her eyes bright. Her voice implored him, "Now Bill, just stay there quietly and try to remember when you last saw your cup!"

He got up from the bed. "What the hell?" he shouted. "What the hell is the fuss about?"

He lowered his voice. "Well I last saw it on the ledge by the cupboard. I had a cup of tea in it," he said guiltily.

Then he saw the marks where his shoes had touched the end of the bed. He brushed at the counterpane. "I should have taken my shoes off, eh?"

Edith was calm now. "So you haven't seen your teacup?" she said, but she could not bear to dismiss the subject, to make an end of it all, without saying, "Your teacup, Bill, the one with the gold, dark-blue and green that hangs on the hook on your shelf?"

Then she suddenly left him, and hurried down the stairs, and knocked sharply on Jean's door, and almost before she was invited, she opened the door and looked searchingly around the room. Her face was flushed. Her eyes were glistening as if she had been leaning too close to the fire. At first she did not speak but glanced meaningly at one of the kitchen cups which Jean had borrowed for a drink of water.

"Have you seen Bill's cup?" Edith asked, staring hard at the cup of water as if to say, "If you borrow this you might surely have borrowed Bill's cup!"

Jean felt a pang of guilt. She had not seen or borrowed the cup but she felt sure that suspicion rested on her.

"No," she said. "I haven't seen it. Isn't it in the kitchen?"

"No, it's not there."

Edith's voice had a note of desperation, as if the incident had brought her suddenly to the limit of her endurance.

"No, it's not there," she said. She felt like weeping, but she was not going to break down, she had her suspicions of Jean. She looked once more around Jean's room, as if trying to uncover the hiding-place.

"I last saw it," she said, "on Saturday at lunchtime when I washed it. Then I went away to my sister's at Blackheath, as you know, and Bill went away for the weekend, and the family was away. That means you were the only one in the house."

"My friend came," Jean reminded her.

Edith pounced. "Perhaps he used Bill's cup?"

No, Jean told her, he hadn't.

"Well you were the only one in the house from Saturday at lunchtime."

"Perhaps Bill knows where it is?" Jean asked.

Edith's voice quavered. "He doesn't. I've asked him. I said to him, 'Now just sit quietly and remember when you last saw it.'"

"What did he say?"

"He said when he last saw it, there were dregs of tea in it, and it was on the ledge by the cupboard in the kitchen. And that's correct," Edith said triumphantly, "for I washed it— you were the only one in the house with it until Monday, today, and between Saturday and today it vanished. There was your friend of course," she said accusingly.

"Oh, he didn't touch it. I don't know what to do with him, he brings me so much food. And he always writes to tell me when he is visiting me."

"Bill is a typical man," Edith said coldly. "He has no idea what food we (he and I) need. If he did he would buy it, and see to things. And now that he's upstairs at work during the day he can't see me to say whether or not he's coming home to dinner."

Then she made a stifled sound, like a sob. "I don't know where his cup has got to, his teacup."

It seemed that the teacup hanging on its golden hook had contained the last of Edith's hope, and now it was gone, someone had taken it. She suspected Jean. Who was this mysterious friend who came to visit Jean? Jean hadn't discovered this friend until Bill had come to stay in the house. It was all Jean's fault, everything was Jean's fault, Jean was jealous of her and Bill, she had stolen Bill's teacup, his special teacup with the gold, dark-blue and green decorations, and the writing underneath. . . .

For the next few days there was tension between the two women.

Edith left a note before she went to work, "Dear Jean, If you are ironing please will you run over Bill's two towels?"

Jean forgot to iron the towels.

Each evening the same questions and answers passed between them.

"Bill's cup must be somewhere. It just can't vanish. You didn't break it by chance, and put it in the rubbish tin?"

"If I had broken it I would have said."

"That woman from Australia broke the handle of the

other one, if that woman from Australia hadn't broken the other one Bill could be using it now."

"*I* broke the other one."

"Then you could have broken this one as well. But I thought . . . that handle . . . I thought it was the woman from Australia. I tried to emigrate to Australia once. I went as far as getting papers and filling them in. . . ."

She spoke longingly as if emigrating to Australia were another of the good things in life which had been denied her at the last moment, as if it were somehow concerned with the affair of Bill and the lost teacup and never ever walking arm in arm in the park, in summer.

By the fourth day the kitchen had been thoroughly searched and the cup was nowhere to be found. Bill was now spending many of his week-nights away from the house, and the two women found themselves often alone together. They spoke little. They glanced grimly at each other, accusingly.

Sometimes at night in her room in the middle of reading her romantic novel from the library (*Set Fair For France, All My Own, Love and Ailsa Dare*), Edith would break down and weep, she could not explain it, but the disappearance of the teacup was the last straw. She said the phrase to herself, drying her eyes, "The last straw."

Then she chided herself, "Don't be silly. What's the use?" But the people in the novels had everything so neatly provided for them. There was this secretary with the purple eyes and trim figure, and she dined by candlelight with the young director, the youngest and wealthiest director of the firm; everybody was jealous of this secretary; all the men made excuses to visit her at her desk, to invite her out. . . .

Edith was heavily built; she bought a salmon-pink corset once a year; she needed to wear it. Her eyes were gray and chipped, like a pavement. Her back humped.

"I'm ugly of course," she said, as she closed *Love and Ailsa Dare*. "I don't mind that so much now I'm used to it, but the teacup, Bill's cup, who has taken it?"

After the week had passed and the cup had still not been found, and there was no clue to its hiding-place, Edith gave up preparing meals for Bill. She even neglected to go to his room to collect what he referred to as his "mid-week smalls." And the following week, in an effort to cheer herself, she went dancing three times to the Council class, but she found little pleasure in it. She had tried to buy a pair of white satin shoes such as everyone else wore, and when she did find a pair they nipped and cramped her two toes, causing a pain which was so prolonged that she visited the doctor (the one around the corner with his house newly decorated, and his smart car standing outside the gate; everyone went to him) who said to her, "I can do nothing about it, it's your age, Miss Rogers, the best thing is for you to have a small operation which will remove those two toes; it's arthritis, it attacks the toes first, with some patients; the operation is quite quick and harmless."

When Edith came home from the doctor's she burst into tears. Two toes removed, just like that! It was the beginning of the end. They would soon want permission to remove every part of her, they did that sort of thing, gradually, once they began they never knew where to finish.

She stopped going to dancing class. She stayed inside by the electric fire, knitting, and sewing at the sewing machine, pedaling fiercely until her legs ached and she was forced to rest them.

One weekend when she returned from her sister's at Blackheath she found that Bill had changed his lodging, had gone to stay with his friends who kept the pub in Covent Garden. He had gone without telling her, without a word. But he never told people things, he was secretive, he didn't understand, he had been in the Army. . . .

That Monday evening on her way past the shops Edith saw Jean in the grocer's; she was buying food, mountains of it. So much for her mysterious friend, Edith thought, as she hurried home.

The two met later in the kitchen, filling their hot-water bottles.

"Have you been dancing lately?" Jean asked.

"Yes," Edith said. "I go often. In fact I went during the weekend. I had a wonderful time. Smashing. Did your friend come?"

"Yes, my friend came, with stacks of food, look!"

Jean pointed to the bread, fruit salad, ham, which she had just bought at the grocer's.

Then, without speaking much—for what was there to say? —they filled their hot-water bottles and said good night.

And no one ever found the dark-blue, gold, green teacup with the writing ARKLOW POTTERY EIRE DONEGAL underneath, that used to hang—an age ago, it seemed—in the kitchen on the special shelf on the shining golden hook!

flu and eye trouble

It is ten minutes to ten in the morning. Although I got up
at half-past six and meant to begin work earlier than now,
I have not done so. I am merely sitting at my typewriter,
sometimes dreaming, sometimes prodding the keys into saying I am tired I am so tired I am so tired oh god but I am
tired; sometimes sniffing the fumes of the oilstove which
burns with a blue flame if it is functioning correctly, like a
child whose condition can be gauged by the color of its
tongue; dreaming, typing, dreaming again; and always con-
scious that in the next room is the man of the house, my
landlord, who has been absent from work all week and who
lies in bed each morning until eleven o'clock. I know that he
is always unwilling to face the upheaval of morning, the
bustling of busybody light in the sky sweeping up the

cinders remaining from the fires of night. He is ill, I think. He coughs, clears his throat, blows his nose, honk.

I wish my landlord would go to work. How can I write when he is in the next room? Oh I wish they would go away, the people with flu and eye trouble, who persist like the ominous dead, in neighboring rooms, who move furniture, tread carpets, rattle teacups, and play fast and loose with legacies and stock-in-trade assumptions! How I wish they would go away, for I am so tired, so tired, I tell you I am so tired I can hardly keep awake. What shall I do? I am afraid of danger.

Yes, I am afraid of danger.

Soon they will pass a law to get rid of me, for I am what is known as a "burden on the state." I receive National Assistance because wherever I go to work I notice that people have five claws and four folds of eyelid, that feathers are dipped in oil, that skin is naturally waterproof, that secret branding irons are inserted in people's lives, this being known as the Scorched Earth Policy where the enemies face each other with no man's land between where nothing ever grows again.

That is why I receive National Assistance from a tall thin man who carries a worn brief case which he opens, drawing out sheets of paper to study. He is an elderly man. His skin is stained, as if carbon paper has been pressed upon it. Is he only an impression of someone? Have the signatory keys touched him?

I thought I was free. The terrible days drag on and on. My landlord is in the next room, in bed with flu and eye trouble. I did not dream his ailment. I heard him say it, outside yesterday afternoon in the sun while he was snipping blithely at the hedge and the man from next door spoke to him.

"Away from work, Dick?"

"Flu and Eye Trouble."

"There's plenty of it about!"

Then the man from next door flung his navy-blue nylon coat across his shoulder, waved good-by, and went up the road to catch the bus for the Café Exclusif where he works as a waiter; while my landlord continued to snip the hedge, addressing passers-by, naming his ailment if they requested it, otherwise commenting on the weather, cold breeze though Spring in the air, and when he was alone whistling over and over one line from a popular song, number five on the hit parade, and the hedge clippings dropped like transferred pungent afterthoughts upon the pavement for only the little dogs to sniff at.

And I am so tired, so tired, I have never been so tired in my life, so tired that I can hardly sit here typing these words. Why does my landlord not leave the house? Is it really flu and eye trouble? I acknowledge that he coughs, clears his throat, blows his nose, but is he going blind, is a film slowly spreading over his eyes? When he is alone does he sneak a magnifying glass from his pocket, train it upon the surroundings which are gradually becoming more dim and blurred?

What will he mend today?

Yesterday he mended the arm of the vacuum cleaner, extracting peanuts, hazelnuts, hairpins, raisins, silver paper from the crook of its elbow. The day before, he fixed a new washer on the upstairs tap. The day before that he made ten wooden wedges for my windows, strengthened the snapping power of the letter box on the front door, revitalized the zing of the electric bell. So much to mend! Will he have time in his life to mend everything? What will he choose to mend today?

Meanwhile it is after ten o'clock and he lies in bed in the next room, and I cannot work, I am so tired, I cannot rid myself of people who occupy the house, I cannot think of anything but flu and eye trouble and what I shall eat for lunch. Cheese soufflé. And I am afraid. Did I tell you that I am afraid of danger? Any human being who occupies the next room, whether he is alive or dead or merely suffering from flu and eye trouble, is a threat to my sanity, my ordered existence, and that is why each night in the shape of a spider I hang woven traps across my doorway. At all costs I must prevent the entry of the living and the dead into my heart.

the windows

I drink far too much coffee. Every time I believe that a bright idea is approaching and the flicker of thought appears on my private radar screen, I switch off, get up from my chair, go into the kitchen, spread two pieces of bread with butter and raspberry jam, and make myself a cup of coffee. There's nothing like a timely snack for soothing away ideas. You know of course that ideas are dangerous —to themselves and to human beings. They should never be left unattended in sleep nor should they be allowed out unaccompanied after dark. The possession of them is a continual risk which no insurance agent would cover. I can't fool you. The cup of coffee is drunk to soothe away the nothingness of being which attacks like a cramp when I sit here at my typewriter with the green paper before me boasting its continued virginity, and my folders, pencils, diaries lying upon the table. My diary has one week to an opening, Postal Information, Ready Reckoner, Weights and Measures, Holidays and Quarter Days, Calendar Events, Moveable Dates, Easter Day for the next twenty-four years. The Ready Reckoner assures me of safety.

My landlord, his eyes glistening with fear, came hurriedly to my room.

"A Ready Reckoner," he pleaded. "Have you a Ready Reckoner?"

From day to day the calculations involving human debt, crime, punishment, are so enormous that even a one and sixpenny diary converting one farthing up to two shillings per pound to the price per hundredweight is a treasured security. And does it not set out one's future with precision to be allotted so many faint ruled lines for each week's living, to be informed of the Easter Days for the next twenty-four years? In twenty-four years I shall be sixty. Where? In this room with this bed, these chairs, windows?

There are five windows, three alike. The sashes and frames which were painted four years ago are ill-fitting and when the wind blows they rattle and shake so much that I was obliged to put wedges of newspaper between the frames and the glass in order that my sleep might not be disturbed at night and my peace of mind interrupted during the day. I sleep so deeply! I know such peace of mind! I am not a sculpture riddled with decay! My three wide tall windows are draped across the lower half with lace curtains which are washed regularly by my landlady, put through the spin drier, ironed, and replaced the same day, for my landlady realizes that I do not wish to be spied upon. The curtains were washed last Saturday. They are still fresh and clean, not yet speckled with soot and dust. Last Saturday I cleaned my windows, first using a patent cleanser which my landlady bought at the Ideal Home Exhibition. I operated it from the special bottle with its special device for squirting the pale-blue liquid upon the glass. Then, using two soft cloths which were part of an old seersucker kitchen apron given to me by an elderly woman who wore her brown suède shoes for eleven years after she bought them one summer while holidaying in Scarborough, I rubbed and polished the windowpanes until the fingerprints of the past week's weather had been erased, and there remained no means whatever of tracing either the crime or its perpetrator. The day then sparkled upon my windows. The crocus-tinted winter sun shone guiltlessly. I could see my face in my side of the windows. Bicycle wheels and little black-and-white dogs and tall people seemed to inhabit my room. The day crumbled and frothed with light; my windows remained adamantine, unsolved, gleaming questions.

Now, once a fortnight, on Tuesday mornings at half-past nine, a man in blue overalls arrives on his motorcycle with his blue-painted ladder, his cloths and bucket, to clean the outsides of all the windows of the house. You understand that I am not the only person in the house to live in a room with windows. There are similar windows downstairs in the sitting room where the visitors arrive. I listen carefully for the visitors. I know that if they do not wish to spend all evening with the television, from Robin Hood to the Epilogue near midnight when all is forgiven with a hymn and prayer Innumerable are the Manifestations of Thy Love Oh Lord, then they may always listen to records, talk, play the piano, or entertain themselves by recording their voices on the tape recorder which was given to the little girl, an only child, for her birthday, as dogs are not really convenient as presents because they mess the flower garden and are a nuisance on the road.

"But dogs move. I want something which moves, and has eyes to look at me!"

Not everyone is given the opportunity to explore the visage and behavior of a tape recorder.

When the window cleaner arrives he works diligently for five or ten minutes upstairs and downstairs, and if you were to ask me how long he spends upon each windowpane I could not tell you, though I once noted it with the second hand of my alarm clock on a day when the world was cheating me, overcharging, giving short measure, offering decayed fruit, wilted cabbages.

If there are people at home the window cleaner rings the front doorbell and asks to be admitted to clean the topmost window on the third floor which he cannot reach with his ladder. Then, after he has finished, he writes WINDOWS CLEANED AS USUAL on a piece of paper and jabs the paper upon the light switch in the hall downstairs. Then, taking his bucket, cloths and ladder, he mounts his motorcycle and is gone. He does not clean the windows of any more houses in the street. He comes from afar. He is employed through secret negotiations on frontiers. Sometimes I hear whispers accusing him of blackmail. It is not true, I protest. The only blackmailer I know is Tomorrow's Jealousy with its futile yet cunning command, Break with the Past.

When the window cleaner is gone the clouds walk into my room, the entire day is invading my room. Birds fly against the pane, beating their wings to enter. The waves lap against the faded sashes, and in all the crevices the salt water leaks through and trickles down the walls and on to the floor and deeper than the floor, and the small mice, constrained, pocket-dropping, shelf-sleezing in gray waistcoats with contemporary sartorial trends, rise to the surface of the morning and struggle crisscross to the shore. Night comes. My windows receive the inevitable darkness. I fold my hands over my breasts that hang bare like lanterns in the hedgerow. Then I bolt my door, turn the key in the lock, and sit alone while my windows gloved in darkness seek still to perpetrate the crime of light.

an incident in mid-ocean

In early spring when the days had just given up swallowing themselves at both ends like snakes and had started to display morning and evening lengths of pink light and poison-patterns of cloud, Miss Dolly Abson of Twenty-three Ivanhoe Road S.E.4. took part in an incident which aroused unpleasant comment and rumor in the neighborhood.

She kissed, long and passionately, a little boy, Maurice Cooke, aged eight, who was coming through the school gate at ten past four in the afternoon. Many people noticed her action. They observed her flushed and nervous demeanor. They knew she was not even related to the child.

"Miss Abson gave me a long long kiss," little Maurice said when he arrived home. "Outside the school gates. She wouldn't let me go."

Maurice's father who was a policeman listened intently.

Miss Abson rented a room in his sister-in-law's house. He had heard that she possessed a "mental history," that she was receiving treatment from a psychiatrist at the local hospital. It was just as well, he thought, to look into the matter, to warn Maurice; one never knew; in spite of the modern outlook certain people should not be at large; harmless beginnings . . .

Miss Abson lived alone in a room on the second floor. She did not go out to work because contact with people worried and frightened her and she found it necessary always to build tall fires around her camp to ward off the beasts of prey which nevertheless surrounded her, their eyes gleaming through the woven darkness of the forest leaves.

Her hands were gnarled with digging moats and destroying bridges. Arrows which were aimed at her window were deflected by the unyielding glass and sometimes re-entered the hearts of those who had shot them.

Miss Abson had no friends. Her only recreations were walking to and from the shops and once a week, on an adventurously long journey which included three sets of traffic lights and one Ring Road, visiting the main local Library where she crept timidly from Sociology to Literature and History, hiding herself behind the tall shelves. Only rarely did she go to the Museums, for one time an officious attendant had taken her umbrella, her coat and handbag, and she had stayed the whole afternoon, terrified and stranded, in the shelter of the History of the Horse.

Therefore she chose to remain most of the time in her room. Her most frequent visits were to her psychiatrist at the hospital not far away. For these visits to him she wore her best clothes, her twin-set and terylene skirt, and changed her underwear. She touched her lips with Pond's Natural Lipstick and rubbed in the hollow of her throat, behind her ears, and on her wrists, next to her pulse, a tiny dab of cream perfume, Lily of the Valley. She brushed her hair with Trill which came in a tube and contained "a replacement of natural oils." Her psychiatrist sat in a room which had two chairs, a desk, a couch, and pot plants arranged along the window sill. He said, "Good morning. How are you, Miss Abson?"

Miss Abson was so lonely. Once when she looked out of her window she saw a little brown dog scratching at the garden. The little brown dog glanced up at her and winked boldly. Miss Abson felt her blood flowing warmly round and round the mulberry bush.

And then, at the beginning of a new term, little Maurice Cooke started school. Miss Abson had seen him at times visiting his aunt, and she had spoken to him and smiled at him. Once, when he called at the house and his aunt was out, Miss Abson brought him up to her room and gave him two foreign stamps with pictures of birds on them. They were birds with red feet standing in a swamp, and a bright blue bird flying in a bright blue sky with the sun like a cherry hanging in the corner and the tall gold grass growing from the earth beneath. They were beautiful foreign stamps. Miss Abson had placed them in a special position on her mantelpiece so that she might look at them whenever she felt lonely, but this day when she had invited Maurice to her room she was overwhelmed by a desire to shower him with gifts. So she gave him her chief treasure of the moment, the beautiful foreign stamps. He clutched them in his hot grubby fingers. He walked backward and forward in the room, trying out the carpet, and then he said abruptly "I'd better go back to school. There's the second bell."

Regretfully Miss Abson showed him downstairs and out the front door.

"Good-by, Maurice."

"Good-by, Miss Abson."

Then, returning to her room, Miss Abson noticed the torn pieces of foreign stamps lying on the carpet. Maurice had torn them while he was walking up and down. Miss Abson tried to stifle her feeling of betrayal and dismay.

He's only a little boy, she thought. I didn't really expect him to appreciate their beauty and value.

Yet her feeling of dismay persisted. Why hadn't he kept the foreign stamps, to love and treasure them?

Later in the week Miss Abson's landlady mentioned that if at any time Maurice rang the doorbell in the lunch hour would Miss Abson please let him in for a few minutes as he was afraid to go to the lavatory at school where the door would not shut and the big boys prowled around after the little boys?

Miss Abson promised to open the door to Maurice.

One lunch hour when she had eaten her cheese on toast and was drinking her coffee and had just started to bite into the Fruitie Bun (threepence halfpenny at the Whip-It Bakery in Ivanhoe Road) the doorbell rang and there was Maurice panting and nearly in tears and with mud all over his legs.

"Miss Abson, I fell in the mud, and there's a big boy after me. He hit me at dinnertime and to pay him back I stirred his custard with my fork and now he's after me."

"Oh dear," Miss Abson said. "Do come in. You know where to clean yourself. You can stay with me until it's time to go back to school."

Then, glancing round in case eavesdroppers were near, she whispered, "If you want to go . . . you know . . . somewhere . . . you can."

Maurice came in and cleaned himself (leaving black shoe polish over his aunt's downstairs carpet) and Miss Abson took him upstairs to her room. What can I give him? she wondered. I should always have something here, ready for when he calls.

She rummaged in an old packet of letters and found a gay postcard from the United States, a relic of Ed Porlock who had been her pen friend in Ohio but who had stopped writing to her, he never said why.

"Here," she said to Maurice. "Here's a postcard. With stamps on it, too."

Then she remembered, with a cry of joy which made Maurice stare at her in bewilderment, that there was a picture card, the Bushy-Tailed Galaco, from the packet of tea. She gave this card to Maurice. I must buy cornflakes in future, she thought excitedly. Cornflakes, and rice bubbles, and all those foods they advertise on television, all the foods with the gifts enclosed in the packets.

Miss Abson had watched advertisements on television. The small set in her room had been supplied by her landlord when in consultation with his wife who suspected that Miss Abson suffered from "mental trouble" they had decided that a television set would be company for her.

"She needs company," they said.

But after watching a few programs Miss Abson had grown tired of television. It made too many demands on space and time; it interfered with thinking, and people on the screen were always smiling with false smiles which said, I know what you are up to, there in your bedroom, Miss Abson; also the characters flitted back and forth so dizzily, with shots ringing out; and the ladies had microphones in their bosoms, and their dresses were covered with scales, like mermaids; and the advertisements with their gift vouchers and giant double-sealed packs were so confusing. . . .

Maurice thanked Miss Abson for the postcard from the United States, and having forgotten about the big boy who was after him and into whose custard he had poked his fork, he went happily back to school. Miss Abson gave him an apple to eat on the way, a rosy juicy apple.

A few days later Maurice brought two of his friends with him in the lunch hour, and Miss Abson invited them all to her room. Oh dear, what had she to give them? Ah! Hadn't she bought a Free Offer tube of toothpaste with a magnifying glass attached? Oh, where was it? And where was the tiny magnet which had taken her fancy in Woolworth's and which she had slipped into her bag when no one was looking? She could find neither the magnifying glass nor the magnet. Her face was flushed with the excitement of looking, lifting up papers, delving in corners, trying to remember, but it was no use, she could not find the gifts.

Then Maurice came up to her. "We've got something for you," he said. "We got it in a penny surprise packet."

He held up a tiny plastic skeleton.

Miss Abson was delighted. "Oh," she gasped. "How clever! How kind! Don't you want it for yourselves?"

"We've got plenty," Maurice said, like a millionaire. "You have it."

Thanking him, Miss Abson took the skeleton. And when Maurice and his friends had gone she propped the tiny white skeleton on her mantelpiece, as her latest treasure.

"Why," she said, "Even its ribs are showing, and all the bones. How clever! Now if Maurice were to grow up to be a doctor he could be studying anatomy even now, identifying and counting the bones in this tiny skeleton! What if he decides to become a doctor? A psychiatrist perhaps!"

Miss Abson felt excitement surging through her. All kinds of plans tumbled through her head, whirling like washing in a washing machine.

And what if he grows up to be a scientist? Oh, Miss Abson

thought, I wonder if my National Assistance grant is enough to buy one of those small microscopes so that Maurice can use it when he calls in the lunch hour? I wonder does he collect stamps? What books does he read? What toys does he play with? He owns a scooter—yes, I have seen him on Saturday mornings with his red scooter—or, perhaps, what about buying him a telescope? An astronomer! A member of the Royal Society!

Miss Abson grew quite dizzy planning Maurice's future, there were so many opportunities for him. When he came to the house now she questioned him closely about his school work and was disappointed when he showed no interest.

"He will grow to it," she said to herself. "There is all the time in the world for him. I wonder will he be a psychiatrist and sit in a room with pot plants along the window sill?"

And that afternoon she put on her best clothes as usual and went to visit her psychiatrist who sat aloof in his white coat and murmured, "Yes, I see, I understand how you feel."

Sometimes she longed to break her psychiatrist into pieces, like a biscuit, and see the icing in between; or to startle him so that his true self rose like a cloud of bees from the secret hive. She did not tell him about Maurice, how she was carefully planning his future, and how she felt so grieved when he did not seem to be aware of the plans being made for him, and was spending valuable time merely playing with his new bicycle and his set of toy trains.

Miss Abson now divided her life between her psychiatrist and Maurice. She thought continually about them both, and dreamed of them, but one night in her dreams when she gave her psychiatrist a tiny magnifying glass marked FOREIGN VALUABLE he stamped his black-polished shoe on it and smashed it to pieces, and Miss Abson woke up crying.

One day Maurice fell on the pavement outside and bruised

his knee. Miss Abson's face went white with shock. She bandaged his wound and insisted that he lie down on her bed. Pleased at the attention, he lay on the bed, crushing the clean counterpane which the landlady supplied, by tradition, for the springtime and summertime; a floral cotton, with roses. Only the day before the landlady had exchanged the somber maroon cover for the bright cotton, with the remark, "Spring is on the way, doesn't it make you feel different? You'll want to get out and about more these spring days, won't you, Miss Abson?"

The landlady was troubled that Miss Abson stayed in her room and did not "mix."

One day when Miss Abson was saying good-by to Maurice at the door he requested, "Kiss Me!"

Startled, Miss Abson laughed nervously, and did not kiss him but pressed him to her affectionately, then said a hurried breathless good-by. I wonder, she thought, did he notice my embarrassment? It was a simple request on his part. I hope I didn't make him think that kissing is something . . . strange. I hope I didn't seem too embarrassed.

Miss Abson was not used to kisses. She was overtaken with sudden gaiety. She went up to her room and opened the windows top and bottom to let in the spring air. She stayed by the window. She did not try to escape. The sun's penetration included her. She blushed and laughed and then, suddenly, an awful thought came to her.

What if Maurice goes home and says, innocently, "Miss Abson kissed me today?" Won't they think there is something strange? I must keep away from the child. I definitely must keep away from the child.

A heavy depression came over her. She closed the windows. And the next day she stayed in bed with a cold, and the lodger who lived on the third floor went to the chemist's for her and returned with a bottle of medicine and a packet of tablets. The medicine was bright pink, such a pretty color; it cheered Miss Abson considerably to take medicine which was such a gay color. She measured for herself the required dose, punctually and carefully, and took the tablets four times during the day, in water, after food.

Near the end of the week when she had recovered a little, she got up and dressed, and rearranged her room, moving the bed to the opposite wall and the bookshelves to the corner near the window. The rearrangement pleased and soothed her. She felt happy again. The day was warm and fine with a fresh breeze blowing.

So she decided to take a walk. She walked up the road near the school, and it just happened that as she passed the gates there was Maurice on his way home.

"Miss Abson!" he shouted, running up to her. She felt excited at this public acknowledgement of herself.

"Kiss me," Maurice pleaded, when he reached her. Now if I refuse, Miss Abson thought, it may seem strange. She laughed nervously.

"No, I'll blow you a kiss," she said, putting her flattened hand primly to her mouth.

"No. Kiss me."

So suddenly she leaned forward and kissed him, then took him in her arms and pressed herself to him, clutching him desperately as if he were her tiny rescuer in the middle of a lonely ocean. And that was when quite a crowd gathered to observe Miss Abson.

"Carrying on like that in the street, too, and she's no relation to him," someone remarked.

Miss Abson still visits her psychiatrist. He still wears his white coat, and nods his head and murmurs, I see, I understand, I know how you feel. And when Miss Abson returns from the hospital she takes off her best clothes and her best shoes and puts on her old ones again, and sits in her chair by the window, looking at the people, and the dogs, and the cats balancing along the brick walls, and the cars passing.

And each day the waves lap against Miss Abson's world and the tide rises higher, over the floor and the baseboard and the table top and the television set and the mantelpiece where the two new foreign stamps lie unclaimed. They have pictures of birds on them, a swamp bird with red legs and a bright blue bird flying through a bright blue sky with the sun hanging like a cherry in the corner and the grass tall and gold growing beneath from the earth.

And soon all is submerged in the tide, and drowned.

the advocate

If you stop Ted in the street and ask him the way he is always eager to direct you. He helps the aged, the blind, the crippled. He will rescue children in distress separated from their mothers in a crowd. At the scene of an accident he is among the first to restore calm, to comfort people, ring for ambulances, distribute hot sweet tea.

He will reprimand or report to the police anyone making himself a public nuisance or breaking the law. Ted has deep respect for the law.

If you say good morning to him he returns your greeting with a cheerful smile.

That is Ted.

At work he is willing, eager; he goes out of his way to please, he stays behind in the evenings to give extra attention to his tasks and prepare for the following day. How courteous he is, how efficient.

In his conversation he refers to his many friends, to his popularity among them.

"They will do anything for me," he says.

He tells you of the liftman at work who is always ready to take him to any floor, to give him service before all others; of the manager who calls him by his Christian name and gives him a friendly wink from time to time, there being definite understanding between them; of the Director who chats intimately with him in a manner which he does not adopt with the other members of the staff; of the shy young office girls who are delighted to be taken "under his wing"; of the Chief Security Officer who, relaxing the principle of keeping aloof from the staff, invites him to his room for coffee, talking to him as an equal.

He likes to make it known that he is given certain privileges: he is allowed free time whenever he chooses; he is trusted, taken into the confidence of others, consulted on personal problems. He has so many friends. If you spend enough time with him you soon learn that he seems to have more friends than most people; you learn too of his illustrious relatives, of famous people who have spoken to him or corresponded with him, of high-ranking officials in other countries whom he has known intimately. In case you do not believe him (but who would doubt his word?) he has a supply of anecdotes, dates, Christian names. And in all his stories he features as the man with many friends, the man to whom people turn for advice and comfort.

Then why is he so alone? Why does he go to bed each night hoping for immediate sleep to ward off his loneliness? Why does he go every Sunday afternoon to the pictures and sit alone in the dark through two showings of the program, and then return to his deserted flat and once more go to bed, trying to evade the loneliness?

He hasn't a friend in the world, and he knows it.

When his back is turned they label him bumptious, overbearing, conceited, nosey-parker, poke-nose, opinionated, bigoted. . . .

Over his body, before he is taken to be buried in the grave of a suicide, they praise him as helpful, kind, courteous, willing, conscientious, a noble and good man. . . .

Which judgment is correct? Is there a correct one? How can one be judged truly unless, like Ted, one hires the services of the Advocate Death?

the chosen image

In late winter when the seed catalogues were thrust through the letter box, the poet, having a spare hour or two, gathered them upon his table, studied them carefully, and from the many magnificent illustrations he chose the bloom which he had decided to plant in a wooden box upon his window sill, for he did not possess a garden. That same afternoon he went to the local post office and after waiting in the queue which extended from the stationery beyond the frozen foods to the cheeses which were next to the door, the poet bought a postal order for two and threepence, put it in an envelope with the number of the packet of seed, and sent it to the seed company. Then he returned home and for three days waited impatiently for the seed to arrive. At night after he had gone to bed he would take the catalogue and read it, and on the third night when he was gazing at the picture of his chosen seed which he already loved very dearly, he happened to read the small print beneath the advertisement.

"Hothouse bloom only," he read.

For a moment he was alarmed. He knew that his room would not provide much warmth for the plant, because he did not earn much money as a poet, in spite of the occasional television interviews where he was asked, What do you think of the world situation? Do you think Success comes too early in this modern age? If you had to live your life over again which one thing would you change? And in spite of the occasional poem printed in a literary journal, and the advertisement jingle which he wrote for a friend in an agency, his slight income did not allow for central heating. How would a hothouse bloom ever survive? he wondered.

"Well," he said at last to himself, "I will breathe on it. My body is warm, well stoked, blood flows from rafter to basement and even the rats have been driven inside this winter to seek shelter in me. By the way, one day when I am free of dreams and light, hawkers, carrion crows and enchantments I shall take time to sprinkle an appetizing sweet poison for the rats in my sealed cabinet. In the meantime I shall await my packet of wonderful blossom."

So he waited, sitting down to work the next morning with his mind continually straying to the thought of growing a hothouse bloom upon his window sill.

In due course the packet of seed arrived. The poet planted it, following the instructions as carefully as his individual temperament would allow. He resolved to breathe upon the soil, the seed and the resulting plant as often as he remembered or was free to do so when he took time from writing his poems to walk about the room counting the faded leaves upon the carpet or looking from the window at the man in the battered gray cap who walked from door to door asking, "Have you any old watches, old gold, bracelets, wedding rings?"

The poet was not married, although like all poets he possessed an invisible muse, a mistress and wife to him, and a wedding ring with which he pledged his devotion to the Chosen Image. Unfortunately, when he turned the wedding ring three times upon his finger it did not provide him with a poem. There had been much controversy. Some poets had said that the wedding ring should provide poems in this way.

Nor could the poet give to the man in the gray battered cap any old watches, old gold or bracelets. How could he possess such valuables? He lived in a small flat where his only treasures which were yet not his alone but were accessible to all, lay arranged in dictionaries and grammars upon his bookshelves. Strange, wasn't it, that no burglar had been known to raid the premises in order to steal suitcases of words?

As for old watches, well, the poet owned a wrist watch which he preferred to keep in his pocket or upon his table. Strapped on his wrist it reminded him of a too genial handcuff to which he had no key, for which no key had yet been made.

Did I tell you that he was a poet who could not write good poetry (there are many such) but unearthed clichés as if they were archaeological treasures arranged on a silver spade? After he had written each poem he was pleased with it, he confused the warmth and excitement which the act of writing gave him with the feelings naturally provided by a thing of beauty; therefore he thought his poem beautiful, and was most distressed and could not understand when later, from somewhere in the cave roof, the dampening idea leaked through that his poem was bad. Yet he could not stop writing just as he could not stop counting the leaves on the carpet or looking from his window at the man calling for Old Watches, Old Gold, Bracelets; or breathing warmth upon the tender leaves that had sprung from his chosen seed.

One evening when he looked at the plant he noticed a tiny bud with its petals beginning to open, and he knew that when morning came the plant would be in full blossom. So he went quickly to bed, pulling the blankets well over him in the belief that concealment means escape and acceleration of time, and soon he was fast asleep and dreaming, but the anonymous voices which inhabit all dreams said to him, "What can you call entirely your own? You cannot write a poem without using the words, often the thoughts, of others. The words of the world lie like stagnant water in the ponds for the poets masquerading as the sun to quench their thirst, spitting out the dead tadpoles and the dry sticks and stones and bones. If ever you have precious thoughts of your own which do not lie accessible to all beneath the sky, how can you safeguard them? Where are your security measures for putting thoughts under lock and key?

"But then, no thoughts belong entirely to you. You have no talent for your work. Your only talent and personal possession is breath, and yet since late winter when the seed catalogues were thrust through your letter box you have bestowed your breath upon a mere plant in order that it should give you pleasure by blossoming on your window sill. Do you think that is wise? Should you not conserve your breath, issue it according to a planned system of economy, and not waste it upon objects like flowers which perish almost as soon as they have bloomed?"

The poet heeded the voices in his dream and the next morning when he looked at the plant, although he knew that the flower was almost in blossom, he refused to breathe upon it, and all day it shivered upon the window sill, feeling for the first time the bitterness of the March winds that moaned up and down the street, and the chill touch of the tendrils of frost and fog that crept down the chimney, under the door, and through the top of the window into the poet's room. And the petals of the flower never opened, their promise was never fulfilled. By nightfall the leaves had blackened at the edges and the bud was a shriveled silken cocoon of nothing.

The saddened poet gazed at the corpse of his Chosen Image, then uprooting it from the window box and taking it outside onto the landing, he thrust the plant and flower down the chute which extended from the top floor to the basement and which carried away all the refuse of the block of flats where he lived—cataracts of detergent packets, drums, soup tins, sardine keys, torn letters, parcel wrappings, newspapers, ends of bread, eggshells, orange peel, used cotton wool. Sorrowfully the poet watched the plant join its traveling companions, finding its place almost as if it belonged there, taking up the new rhythm of its journey, jostling, struggling in the narrow chute, being trampled and crushed by overbearing jam jars, bottles, and a rusted paraffin container.

For a moment the poet regretted his action. He longed to be in his room again with the plant there on the window sill, almost in blossom, and with him breathing tenderly upon it to provide it with the warmth it needed in order to survive.

Then he shrugged, and smiled cheerfully. What was the use of feeling dejected when one had only done what was right, and refused to waste one's breath upon a negligible hothouse bloom which had been deceitful anyway as its real nature had not been known until the small print of the contract was studied?

"I will forget the whole episode," the poet said.

And he tried to forget.

He returned to his room and began to write his new poem. Now and again he glanced at the empty window box and sighed. The poem refused to be composed. The poet turned his wedding ring three times. Still the poem refused to be composed.

Well, that was nothing unusual.

He glanced once again at the empty window box and stilled his conscience by remarking to himself, "Anyway it was a hothouse bloom and would never have survived the rigors of this climate; not even if it had been allowed to blossom. It was not selfish of me to deny it my breath, to dispose of it. Rather was it an act of thoughtfulness which is rare these days."

He smoothed the paper before him, ready to imprint his poem.

Then a fit of coughing seized him, and he died.

In her silk and ivory tower the Muse turned from her window. "He was a hothouse plant, anyway. I chose him at random without reading the small print at the bottom of the contract. He would never have blossomed. In future I shall keep my breath to myself—well at least I shall not be tempted when aspiring poets thrust their souls catalogued, numbered, illustrated, through my letter box."

the linesman

Three men arrived yesterday with their van and equipment to repair the telephone lines leading to the house opposite. Two of the men stayed at work in the house. The third carried his ladder and set it up against the telegraph pole twenty-five yards from the house. He climbed the ladder and beyond it to the top of the pole where, with his feet resting on the iron rungs which are embedded at intervals in the sides of the pole, he began his work, his hands being made free after he had adjusted his safety harness. He was not likely to fall. I did not see him climb the pole. I looked from my window and saw him already working, twisting, arranging wires, screwing, unscrewing, leaning back from the pole, dependent upon his safety belt, trusting in it, seeming in a position of comfort and security.

I stared at him. I was reluctant to leave the window because I was so intent upon watching the linesman at work, and because I wanted to see him descend from the pole when his work was finished.

People in the houses near the telegraph pole had drawn their curtains; they did not wish to be spied upon. He was in an excellent position for spying, with a clear view into the front rooms of half a dozen houses.

The clouds, curds and whey, were churned from south to north across the sky. It was one of the first Sundays of spring. Washing was blowing on the clotheslines in back gardens; youths were lying in attitudes of surrender beneath the dismantled bellies of scooters; women were sweeping the Saturday night refuse from their share of the pavement. Perhaps it was time for me to have something to eat—a cup of coffee, a biscuit, anything to occupy the ever marauding despair.

But still I could not leave my position at the window. I stared at the linesman until I had to screw up my eyes to avoid the bright stabs of spring light. I watched the work, the snipping, twisting, joining, screwing, unscrewing of bolts. And all the time I was afraid to leave the window. I kept my eyes fixed upon the linesman slung in his safety harness at the top of the telegraph pole.

You see, I was hoping that he might fall.

the salesman

It was two weeks before Christmas. The salesman with his battered suitcase was walking from door to door offering his Christmas cards. It was raining. I know that the cards were stained and streaked with rain, that the dye was running from the satin ribbons of the sample cards, that the salesman's muddy fingerprints had trespassed indelibly across the snow scenes and the silver-clad angels. I watched intently from my window. I could not keep my eyes from the salesman. I knew it was bitterly cold outside; I was glad to be indoors with a cheerful fire burning, and although I felt cold enough to move nearer the fire I still could not leave my place at the window. I watched the salesman walk to each front door, ring the bell or bang the knocker. I watched the door open and the householder shake her head, Nothing today thank you, no we have our Christmas cards thank you, we bought them in November, Woolworth's had them in November. . . .

While the salesman made his calls he left his shabby case against the fence or wall of each house, and took only a handful of samples to the door. I observed him so carefully. Time after time heads were shaken and his offers of sale were refused. When he reached the end of the street he had sold nothing. It was still raining. Smoke from the chimneys mingled with the rain that fell in black drops, like a stained meal poured through the air and swallowed by the world, to locate and highlight its disease.

The salesman's clothes were ragged. He kept turning up his collar against the rain, and rather than keep opening his suitcase he tried to shelter his few samples inside a frayed pocket of his overcoat. I could not stop myself from watching him.

When he approached each door I trembled with suspense as he offered his cards. I waited, watching every move of the woman who answered the door. Then, when I saw her shake her head and close the door, I sighed with relief.

No one will buy his cards, I thought with pleasure.

Why did I hate the shabby salesman going from door to door trying to sell his rain-soaked Christmas cards?

How pleased I felt that no one would buy from him!

I have my revenge now, I said to myself, and turning at last from the window I warmed my hands against the fire, my palms held in an attitude of supplication or surrender.

how can I get in touch with Persia?

Early in his life he grew mistrustful of messages borne to him by word of mouth or letter. He became concerned with invisible communications and the sly cryptic evidence of them in telephone wires, radio aerials, valves and switches, and, lately, the four hundred and five invisible lines of a television picture. Electricity fascinated him. When his parents talked of the "old days" of gas lamps in the street and candles burning with their leaf-shaped flame at the foot of the stairs, he felt a special pride in the fact that he had always known electricity, the power of turning the switch and invading the room with probes of light or condemning it to darkness. When his mother plugged in the electric iron he used to rub his finger along the bottom of the iron, collecting the evidence, the mystical vibrations, tracing them along the cord to the unobtrusive three-pin plug above the baseboard, just inside the door. The repeated warnings BE CAREFUL OF ELECTRICITY, THE INVISIBLE KILLER, only increased its fascination. He became preoccupied even in sleep and dreaming with its mystery. He longed to seek out the reality of it, to put his hand into the dark and touch it.

He constructed his first transmitting and receiving set. He was filled with wonder and love at the variety of messages in the air. Sometimes messages came to him even while he was walking in the street or at work. While other boys of his age sought the company of girl friends and found their escape and pleasure in clubs, gangs, the telly, the dance hall, the cinema, he derived his entertainment and solace from the workbench in his tiny room on the top floor of the house where he had an increasing supply of electrical gadgets, wires, plugs, and his transmitting and receiving set. Often he would stay into the early hours of the morning, tapping in code and talking to people in the distant countries which could only be located on the map by searching the index and then carefully trapping the area between its bonds of latitude and longitude. Every country was trapped in this way. Not one could hide or fake death in order to escape notice, such was the ruthlessness of the map of the world.

But all things were ruthless, all men and their instruments. And what of Death?

He used to sit in the dark, sometimes not attending the signals on his wireless, considering the problem of death and the means of solving it with his one ally—Electricity. Then he would switch on the B.B.C. and laugh when the late-night clergyman entreated him to Lift Up Your Hearts

For God Dwells on High, Come Unto Him All Ye that Labor and Are Heavy-laden and He Will Give You Rest. Well, he was not heavy-laden, anyway. He was selected to receive special messages. The sound waves eddied about him, touching his skin, the palms of his hands, caressing him, even underneath his clothing; he throbbed with messages.

He worked as a packer in a Mail-Order Firm at Brixton. He applied for that job after the episode of the sea holiday when the family doctor had said that he needed rest, he had been growing too fast, and now that he was in his early twenties he should be leading a "more normal" life.

Sometimes he stayed in bed all day.

"You great lout," his father said. "When I was your age . . ."

That was when he was working at the self-service store, on the adding machine, for he was interested in numbers and sympathetic to machines. Then for a while he stayed at home while the doctor persisted in telling him to get to the seaside.

But who would supply the money? He grew tired of hearing of the seaside.

For three days and nights without ceasing he communicated with foreign places. He called it his seaside holiday. It refreshed him. Besides, he had a plan in mind. It would astonish the world, it would show everybody. He slept with wires round his wrists to collect and store messages which came while he slept, for it would take much time and study to complete his plan, there was not a moment to be lost because the life expectation of every human being had lengthened and branched out at the edge with poisonous blossoms, wire flowers lit by concealed bulbs which flashed their urgency, red, gold, and dark green.

It troubled him that when he applied for the job at

Brixton he was asked to sign a form stating that he was willing to be searched every evening before he left the factory. Why should he say that he was willing to be searched when he was not willing to be searched? What were they trying to seize from him? He was grateful that his messages, the receiving waves, were invisible, and his heart was learning to beat in Morse code, so as to transmit secret answers, and not a soul at the Mail-Order Firm knew of his secret preoccupations or of his growing power and alliance with electricity.

"Get out and about," his father said, "instead of tinkering and talking to Persia."

So he went one night to the wrestling, and although he listened carefully to the names of the holds—Full Nelson, Drop Kick, Toe Hold, Body Scissors—and tried to grasp the special significance of them when applied to his secret plans, the spectacle of wrestling did not interest him. He had gone there only to please his mother when she said, "Yes, do as your father says, have an evening out, to the stock-car racing or somewhere."

His heart had beaten fast with dread when she said, "or somewhere," for the expression was so vague that he knew she was trying to convey a special meaning, perhaps a warning. Had she intercepted a message intended for him?

Sometimes when he came home at night he found that his father had gone down to the pub and he was alone with his mother. He enjoyed these evenings. He sat in his father's chair by the stove and watched his mother bending and twisting the wire to make the frames of the lamp shades which she afterward fleshed with stiff material, like parchment, painting flowers and scenes and faces upon it. Making lamp shades was her hobby. She had orders from so many people that she could hardly keep up with the demand. Some she gave away, others she sold; it depended. As he sat there watching and talking to her, telling her about the latest messages from Persia, and about his job in the Mail-Order Firm, he would at times be overcome by a haunting fear at the sight of his mother's face and the used look of her skin, as if someone in the Mail-Order Firm had charge of her, stamping wrinkled destinations upon her face in a crude impersonal way, as if she had changed into one of those dull-colored envelopes which are issued by the Post Office with the instructions, RE-USE, ATTACH FLAP AND RE-USE TO ASSIST ECONOMY DRIVE. What did it mean? He would try to forget his fear. He would renew the conversation, giving detailed accounts of his day at work, but when the silences came his mind would be occupied with the problem of destinations, areas of land and their ownership, human mortgages, electricity; chiefly electricity.

When his father returned from the pub, he would stop talking to his mother and get up from his father's chair, and go quickly to his room, close the door carefully, lock it, draw the curtains, and sit at his workbench considering the wonderful prospects of electricity. Once, he heard rumors that his enemies were closing in upon him but he suppressed his immediate panic and smiled with scorn—was not electricity his lifelong ally?

But I need to catch up, he thought, with urgency. I should have studied it from the very beginning. In the medical world it is a miracle. I should have gone on and been a doctor.

Gone on? Where? To Persia?

Splutter, peep-peep, dot-dot-dot.

That was the language which he had learned and which he could now understand more easily than the language of people, of his mother and father. He could hear their murmurs to each other on the stairs, a rustling sound, like a straw broom sweeping debris or other messages of a hard substance, metal or stone, being shaken to extract them from the bottle in which they had drifted thousands of miles across the ocean.

He turned from listening to them and switched on his receiver.

Splutter, peep-peep, dot-dot-dot.

He felt lonely. The language infuriated him suddenly. He switched off and sat on his bed and listened to the B.B.C. Any Questions? Does the Team think? Will the Panel tell me?

"Go on," he said, and lay down on his narrow bed and closed his eyes.

It happened that there was an epidemic of flu in the district. Everybody seemed to be catching it. Some of the workers at the Mail-Order Firm were taken ill, and were sent home, and calling on their doctor on the way home they were put on the panel and given prescriptions for fancy nose sprays, bottles of medicine, boxes of pills.

First his father had flu and recovered.

He knew that he would be immune from it as he needed all his strength for the important work which was to decide his destiny. He realized that he could not be spared from his nightly conversations with far countries, and from the time-devouring problems of electricity.

The flu avoided him, and arrived at his mother. Quite surprisingly she talked in her sleep one night and his father called him, saying stupidly, "Mum's talking in her sleep. She's delirious. We'll get the doctor."

He did not approve of his father's suggestion. He was seized with jealousy which raged in him, making his face turn a violent red and his heart thud and throb against his chest. Why was his father not consulting him, instead of a doctor?

His jealousy subsided, his face paled; his heart was heavy with disappointment. No one knew of his secret qualifications; he would have to take action, prove himself; human lives were in the balance, the entire human race depended upon him. It was time; he would act; how?

The doctor came, after four hours. And by morning his mother was dead.

When he heard the news he went to his room and tuned in to Persia.

His mother was dead. Her unfinished lamp shades lay upon the table, beside the useless twists of copper wire. Her face was at last franked and canceled with free death. Or so the world believed. He could not understand, he could not think clearly. He stayed all that night and the night before the funeral, leaning over his transmitting and receiving set, trying to interpret the new signals which had found their way amongst the splutter, peep-peep, dot-dot-dot.

The day of the funeral was as sunny as Bank Holiday, and the ride to the cemetery had a festive air about it, with the hearse speeding along so that his mother might keep her last appointment.

But his mother disliked appointments; she had never kept them; and this was not her last, oh no, oh no. He burst out laughing in the back of the car.

"It takes people in different ways," his father said.

"We all need a good cry," said his aunt from Liverpool.

And when he saw them lowering his mother's coffin into the grave he still did not cry, and after the funeral he went straight home and got in touch with Persia.

He was talking to Persia, and trying to understand the complexities of the strange new code when he conceived his plan. When his father, as had been arranged, went north to Liverpool to stay with the aunt, he would be alone in the house. That was his opportunity.

Two days later he hired a Self-Drive car. He drove in the evening to his mother's grave, dug up her coffin, opened it, removed his mother's body which he wrapped in a blanket and laid gently in the back of the car.

He kissed his mother. He began to cry. "Don't worry," he said. "I've never believed it. Even when they wanted to search me to take my life away from me, I've never believed it. All the messages have proved it is not true. There is no death, now that I have solved the mystery. You did not guess, did you, that I had solved the mystery, all this time in my room with the copper wire and switches and a few strips of aluminum? I'm going to bring you back to life. You can't die, not any more; besides, the people are waiting for their lamp shades to protect them from the light, all up and down the street they are waiting for their lamp shades, and soon you'll be making them, and I'll be sitting by the stove, watching you, talking to you."

He drove the car home, and carried his mother to her room, and laid her on his bed. Far into the night he worked to attach the wires and switches to her body. She lay with gold and silver insect-scaffolding over her; like Gulliver wired to earth by the little people.

"She is regaining her strength," he said confidently, distributing wires, locating switches, placing a light bulb on her breast.

At half-past three in the morning he made a cup of tea on the gas ring in the corner of his room. He offered the tea to his mother, first taking a few sips to test whether it was too strong or too sweet as she did not fancy it that way. She did not move. She did not even raise her head to drink the tea. He switched on the electric current. A slight shock trembled through his fingers and along his arm as he touched the network of wires, but still his mother did not move. He drank the tea himself. Then he kissed the cold gray face; there was a blue tinge under the skin, like deep water. He crumbled a piece of Rich Tea Biscuit over the mouth in the hope that her tongue would dart forth, like a lizard's tongue, and seize it. But there was still no movement. He rechecked the wires and the switches. His face was dazed and pale; his cheekbones felt massive, seized by a clamp; his mouth was dry.

"She is regaining her strength," he repeated.

He sighed. He found another blanket, and lay beside his mother on the narrow bed. "When I count twenty," he said to himself, "she will come alive."

He counted twenty; she was not breathing.

"If I hear a motor bike while I am counting fifteen, and if the edge of the curtain moves during the following fifteen and the light from the street lamp outside shines in a slit upon the wallpaper, then she will be alive. He counted fifteen, listening anxiously for the motor bike, and opening his eyes to observe the patch of wallpaper where the street lamp would shine.

He heard a motor bike. A wind blew the edge of the curtain, letting in the light. But nothing persuaded his mother to wake.

"It takes time," he said, his heart heavy with the humiliation of needing to include motor bikes, numbers, street lamps, in his perfect plan, to rely on ordinary visible objects when the secret world of electricity was under his command, as his agent and slave.

He drew another blanket over him and slept. He lay there for two days, never entirely losing his faith in the power of the electricity, but relying more and more upon chance happenings, shadows, noises, radios in the next house, to influence his mother, to compel her to wake. But the motor bikes, the lorries, cars, roared up and down the street; shadows formed and dissolved and the light made patterns on the wallpaper; and his mother stayed dead. From time to time he still switched the current on and off in the hope of reviving her.

It only needs time, he thought. A season, a spring or summer.

His head felt unearthed, ancient, like the skull of a mammoth. Drums beat in the sky; his skin was too tight, it would not fit.

At three o'clock the next afternoon when the man from the Self-Drive Hire Company called, knocked, and got no answer, when neighbors saw the accumulating milk bottles outside the door and the paper boy found his papers not collected, when the world, as it does in a feat of intensely interested arithmetic, put two and two together, the police were called. They forced an entry to the house. They searched. When they came to his room they found his mother lying on the bed, laced with wires and switches. He was leaning over the transmitting set in the corner of the room. Tears were streaming down his face. He was trying to get in touch with Persia.

a relative of the famous

If you happen to be a relative of the famous you are granted certain concessions and privileges, although you understand that your claim or the claim of others on behalf of you must first be recognized. Imposters are frowned upon. The question is, how does one decide in the first place which of the famous are imposters?

After death is best; time, sprung free of the trap, exercises itself day and night in long division, subtraction, blinding itself in the poor light of the grave where the little worms patrol the corridors carrying torches past each darkened room.

The remainders are framed in gold.

Now there was once a woman painter who became famous after her death when bearded men plunged swords in each other's hearts to possess one of her paintings or to donate one, suitably inscribed and recorded, to the local gallery which was dark brown, opening and closing with a faulty catch, like a broom cupboard where in spring and summer the dust is elbowed away and the shapes of paint are temporarily revived, with the sun warming the creaking damp joints of color, the drip-dry bones of light blazing.

Now after the death of the painter, after her biography had been written, the memoirs of her friends printed and her work appraised as successful communication, a tunnel through dense mountain walls where the penalties of work are loneliness, suffocation, drowning in underground streams, pit-blindness, those who recognized her work and were grateful for human routes at any cost, for burdened ants who never swerve, decided to extend their interest.

"Has she any relatives?" they asked.

"None," was the answer.

Then suddenly they heard of Wilfred, the nephew, the eccentric beachcomber with the encyclopedic knowledge of flora, fauna, conchology.

They were amazed and excited.

"Why didn't someone tell us before?" they cried. "To think that Wilfred has been living all this time in a remote northern seaside town, and not a word has been breathed that he was a relative of the famous!"

Few people knew.

"Wilfred?" they said. "Dirty, evil, wandering day and night along the beach gathering shells, naming them like dynasties, tracing their kingdom.

"Wilfred feeds on the sea.

"But that is not all. Look at him standing day after day in the main street outside the Post Office, abusing people, throwing stones through the letter boxes."

It is one of the most insulting acts possible to stand outside a Post Office, cursing and throwing stones!

Wilfred smelled like a decayed forest; he would have to be put away soon, everyone knew where, behind high walls where day and night are striped and the sun sets with the porridge in a little white china bowl.

But when Wilfred was discovered to be a relative of the famous, everything was all right; they did not put him away, there was no one to pry and ask if he knew where he was and what was his name; instead they gave him a Social Security Allowance which came in a clouded blue envelope every Monday; they let him live in his tiny beach hut by the mud flats and the gray mangroves, and those who were interested no longer spoke of him as dirty and evil, but they shook their heads, saying, "How sad! How sad, yet fascinating! You know his aunt is the famous painter."

Then they whispered their final remark, "An accident of birth!"

How does one know whose infirmity one carries?

As if birth were a left-luggage department where the parcels sometimes became confused.

And there was Wilfred, with his skin lined with the same substance as that of his aunt, a famous painter—who knows what luggage had been checked in for her to be collected by others, to burden their lives?

But Wilfred did not heed these searching discussions. Wilfred was enclosed in his own world. He was not a dung beetle or mole making person to person calls through dangerous territory; his life contained enough peril. Wandering the beach gathering shells, cursing and throwing stones in the main street remained his right and privilege.

Now a rich woman of esteem lived in the town. She was shaped like a sonnet, with piled white hair. She planned her life and the lives of others; she could afford to, for much wealth is required for planning. She contributed generously to the Church, the Red Cross, the Mothers' Union, the

Women's Division of the Farmers' Union, but her particular interest was directed to the famous, many of whom she knew personally, and although her husband who was also a person of esteem liked to be private, sitting in his armchair, wearing an old gray cardigan of humility, she preferred her intimate knowledge of the famous to be made known. You can imagine her surprise and the quickening of her interest when she learned that Wilfred, a relative of the famous, was living almost on her own doorstep.

"In the same town, I can hardly believe it!" she exclaimed with delight.

"To think that we have been living here all this time, and never known about Wilfred!"

She invited Wilfred to tea.

He accepted the invitation. He came to her house at five o'clock one evening (though it was impossible to tell how he knew the exact time) and stood all evening in the center of her living room, his blue eyes wide, the curses flowing from his lips, brisk, playful, terrible, like sporting sharks in summer waters. The curses tore the esteemed woman's flesh to pieces; she looked embarrassed and went to find the Elastoplast with the built-in dressing. And still the curses flowed! And Wilfred was not even standing in the main street outside the Post Office! But they served him tea and smiled at him and listened to him, yet they were relieved when he began to glance anxiously around the room, as if it were time for him to go home. He grew suddenly quiet. Not once had he smiled in answer to their smiles. Then he spoke the esteemed woman's name.

"Mrs. Allcloud," he said. "Between the cat's-eyes, the cockle, the fan shell, the lamp shell, stars that may brag may brag."

"How delightful," she said, trying to concentrate. "Well, you'll be on your way I suppose, Wilfred."

She spoke as one might to a traveler who was leaving for a long night's hazardous journey through frost and fog.

Wilfred put down his teacup which he had held all evening, and without saying Thank you or smiling good-by he went from the room, along the passage, and out the front door.

Mrs. Allcloud followed him to the door. "Good night, Wilfred."

He did not look back. He walked along the road with his head high, his steps mincing, if by mincing one means that footsteps grind the flesh of the earth, churning it into little heaps like worm casts.

"Well," Mrs. Allcloud sighed, returning to her living room and mending with one wholesome knitting glance the cracks in the windows, walls, roof, made by an evening of well-directed curses. "He didn't say Thank you, or seem pleased. His manners are frightful. But we must learn to understand him, mustn't we, Anthony?"—she glanced apprehensively at her husband and fear looked through the lines of her rhyming body—"We must understand him, cultivate him, for poor Noeline's sake. It is sad that I missed making her acquaintance, but I recognized from the first the value of her art, I was on the committee, remember, who chose her painting for the gallery, and though there was a storm, with the public labeling the painting as obscene, I stood firm. Poor Wilfred! It is not as if he were *nobody!*"

And the next day, having spread her evening's memory with golden syrup, Mrs. Allcloud talked gaily and brightly at the Ladies' Club, mentioning, only by the way, that Wilfred (nephew of the famous artist) had visited her for tea, that she knew him well, that he was a close friend of the family.

And in future, every month, sometimes twice a month, she made a point of inviting Wilfred to tea. She would stop him outside the Post Office where he was engaged in his curses. He would pause when he caught sight of her.

"Building negotiations!" he would shout. "The lowest or any tender not necessarily accepted!"

She would smile kindly.

"Will you come to tea, Wilfred, on Saturday evening at five?"

"As a dome of shells is ground to sand, soft bodies within, the resentment of water against temples, give a dog a bone a bone to carry home, to bury—purport, purport, fangs, change, prayer to pulp. . . ."

"Will you come to tea? Fifty-five East Street."

It was as well for him to be reminded of the address.

Then she would smile at him once more, and he would stare with his blue eyes unsmiling, then resume his fury against the Post Office.

But he always accepted the invitation to tea, behaving on each occasion as he had done the first evening. Once, though, he brought Mrs. Allcloud a mountain orchid which he had gathered from the bush-clad hill overlooking the sea.

Mrs. Allcloud flourished with goodness and interest.

"His aunt," she would say, "the famous painter, you know . . ."

"Have you read her biography, the definitive edition?"

"Have you read her collected letters?"

Once when someone remarked that no mention was made of Wilfred in the biography, she said warmly, "I am so fond of Wilfred. You know how he is, but somehow one can sense the family trend, underneath everything he is gifted, so gifted."

"You remember the famous painter? I know her nephew, he often comes to tea."

The one flaw in Mrs. Allcloud's happiness at this time was

her inability to mold Wilfred's life, to plan for it as she had done for so many others. She had helped artists by giving them money, buying their pictures. She had encouraged writers, subscribed to the publication of their books. She longed to help Wilfred in some way, to possess him, to stake her claim in his life. She had never been faced with anyone like Wilfred. He was a mountain wall, she could make no impression on him, her fingerprints, her footprints did not show; his secret inward weather covered all her tracks.

It was a serious and disturbing occasion when Mrs. Allcloud discovered that Wilfred was not after all a relative of the famous. She had been studying more closely the family history of the painter. She realized that somehow a mistake had been made, that Wilfred was no relation at all, that he belonged to the South Island Vincents, the Racing People in Southland, a notable family certainly, but no connection, no connection at all with the famous painter. She still felt bound by her conscience to invite Wilfred to tea—he was so helpless, so strange, what could one do?—but the filth of his unwashed body and clothes appalled her, and his curses, there in her living room, were an abuse and insult which no sensitive person, like herself, could be expected to endure. And he showed no gratitude for the interest in him, he made no response to sympathy and kindness. There had been the gift of the mountain orchid; certainly that had been touching, but now, seen in its proper perspective the encouragement and cultivation of Wilfred had not been altogether wise.

But Mrs. Allcloud kept her discovery to herself, although she did not make it known now that Wilfred was a relative of the famous. And who was to know? Who was interested enough to delve into the Vincent family history?

Many people were interested. She realized this almost as

soon as she denied it. Her discovery would not for long remain secret. Oh how confusing one's life became, she thought. How could one act for the best, taking all things into consideration?

All things?

Public safety, concern, hygiene, for instance.

And Wilfred?

How could she deal with Wilfred? How can you deal with someone who is less concerned with your presence, your power, your riches, than he is with naming shells, following the tides, cursing and throwing stones in the main street outside the Post Office while the letters flow backward and forward, here and there, with the correct number of stamps on them and the correct address and the enclosed lucid notes between person and person, How pleased I was to visit you on Saturday for tea, how a warmth flows through me when I realize your interest and kindness, your desire to befriend me, whether on behalf of a mythical aunt who laid submarine cables or of myself who am enclosed forever, hermetically sealed, or on behalf of humanity biting its tongue in two, what do I care about your snobbish excuses, when you invite me, befriend me, but I regret I cannot accept your invitation, your life is adrift on the beach, you have gone out with the tide, I am alone in the world, even with daisy chains of aunts who are famous or unknown, I am alone in the world, yet I am the Saviour in the main street, I will defend the whole of humanity against the evils of the Post Office, but help, rescue, what am I to do?

burial in sand

He was going overseas so we buried him that afternoon, shoveling the sand over him with sticks of driftwood. We buried his wife too. They lay under the weight of the sand, protesting, squinting in the brittle yellow light that under the pohutukawa trees burned with a blue gloss. The day hung like blue and yellow plums, a perfect shape, with the light dripping like juice through the sky torn by birds' beaks, hawks' eyes, certain scissor fears raping through the sky. The sound of the firing of shells came from along the cliff, toward Black Bay. Territorials were practicing: we were in a forbidden area.

"We shouldn't be along this way, we might get killed," Len said.

"Nothing would kill us," Colin replied, heaving his burden of sand. Sue, his wife, reached from her golden grave and clasped his fingers in hers. They kissed, with sand getting in their mouths and hair, then with sudden tremendous energy they escaped from their grave and ran together along the beach, shaking the sand from their bathing togs. They entered the water and swam to the Black Rock where they climbed to the highest point, and shouting and screaming with laughter, they hailed Len and me.

"King of the Castle!" they cried. "King of the Castle!"

They swam in shore to us then, and we sat on the sand, listening to the tumult of water, the tiny waves, ear-size, playing hook-and-eye, the heavy-footed surf prowling its beat around the rocks, the escaping sighs, moans, the groaning convict sea dragging its green chains along the sea bed, the cat-hiss, arched white back of stranded foam, the quick old age of the white-topped tide, sprawled on the sand like mouse hair through an uncleaned comb. . . . We listened to the exploding shells at Black Bay, to the sea birds, and to the waves once more which, like us, refused to heed the warning DANGER AREA, LIVE SHELL PRACTICE.

A spray of rocks came flying from the cliff into the water.

Do we know the tides? Len asked.

No, we hadn't any idea of the tides. We could be trapped, unable to climb the steep cliffs, and drowned, and that would be an end of Len and me, and Colin and Sue with their journey overseas. Colin was a painter. He had won a scholarship to Paris, but he had contrived things so that he and Sue would be living most of their time in Spain in what he called "the Mediterranean light." Colin was going to paint and paint from dawn till dark every day of the year. He aimed to fulfill himself, to discover his true style, whatever that meant, to surprise himself with messages. And Sue, faithful, beautiful, would be by his side always to offer comfort and communion. There would be no children, they said. Not yet, anyway.

We were not annihilated that day by the shell practice or by the invading sea. We dressed, Len and Colin in their old clothes, Sue and I in our summer dresses. The sun had left scorch-marks on our skin, it had been trying to flatten us out, to uncrease us, change us to simple earth shot inch-high by burrowing worms who lie dead, swollen, when the tide enters their door. But we were proofed against the sun. We went home to Len's place, calling at the Mon Désir on the way, for drinks. People were sitting in basket chairs in the garden. They were being Continental, they said, looking self-conscious. The violinist from over the Bay was playing gypsy music.

"All very nice," Len said.

We had a riotous party. Were not Colin and Sue going overseas? Had not Colin's chance come at last? to paint in the daylight hours instead of working on farms, on the wharf, at the freezing works, rabbiting, all the laboring jobs with high wages but with darkness, utter darkness at the end of the day. There were the weekends of course; Colin painted like mad then. Everyone was glad he had been given a chance. Everyone liked him, and now that he was married to Sue they seemed to like him even more.

"They deserve all this happiness," everyone said when news came of the scholarship. They said it without envy; they were glad, they said, to see people getting on, young artists especially. . . .

I did not see them off at the wharf. Len went, said Good-by, Bon Voyage, and the rest of it. We had been close friends with them, and we missed them, we kept talking about them as they had been that day on the beach with the shells firing around us and the tide shattering its prospects, prisms and forebodings on the sand, driving its warhead between the rocks while the blue sky turned its face away, I haven't seen a thing!

From time to time we heard from Colin and Sue. They were not enthusiastic letter-writers, but sent postcards covered with extravagantly happy phrases, and short brilliant notes where each wrote alternate sentences so that the finished message, instead of achieving a happily married unity, acquired a rather frightening anonymity.

"Who's who in Spain?" Len said thoughtfully.

But it seemed that Colin was bursting with inspiration, he was lying in the shallows of dreams, he said, and could see right to the bottom, to the bedrock of sleep and images. . . .

After six months, however, a reticence crept into their notes. Yes, everything was all right, everything was fine, and wouldn't they like to be back with us on the beach, buried in their graves of sand with the sun cooking in the sky and the pohutukawa blossoms lit like sparklers on the Fifth of November, oh wouldn't they like to be back there now!

Colin's scholarship came to an end. They had saved enough to keep them for a while longer, they said. They were living cheaply in Spain. They sent us Christmas cards which said Navidad, Navidad!

"Certainly the light in Spain is good," Len said. He spoke thoughtfully, as if he were arguing with himself and didn't want to win.

"He'll be doing his best work now, I'll be bound." But Len sounded unconvinced, and depressed. He went out to the Mon Désir and sat in a basket chair in the Continental garden, listening to gypsy music and getting drunk on whisky.

When next we heard from Colin and Sue it was many months later. We learned that Colin had found a job teaching English in Barcelona and was earning enough to keep him and Sue and (he said) "any others happening along," while he still had plenty of time for his painting. He was painting large canvasses, he said. He gave their exact measurements.

"Like the weight of a horse, an income tax return, the vital statistics of a woman," Len remarked.

A year passed. We heard no more from Colin and Sue. Friends who had been to Spain said they had met Colin and Sue one day when they were visiting an aquarium, but they gave no further information. Then I too got caught in the craze for traveling overseas. I planned to live on one of the Spanish Islands. I arrived in London, took the train and boat to Paris, traveled down to Barcelona where I had a few hours to spend before I caught the boat to the Balearic Islands. I had written to Colin and Sue, telling them of my plans, and whether they liked it or not they were obliged to offer to meet me at Barcelona and entertain me before my boat sailed. But why should they not want to meet me? Of course they would be pleased, they said. It was just that we had not heard from them for so long except for the Christmas cards which said like a protest, Navidad, Navidad!

The train arrived in Barcelona. All morning along the coast the red earth had swallowed me, the olive trees leaned like gray corrugated switchbacked elephants doomed to take root in the earth; their leaves turned like handfuls of snow in the wind; there were no barriers of light; what propped up the sky?

I climbed from the train, a hazardous journey to the platform. I was standing tuned in to depths of blackness, light, foreign words, substantives which comforted the objects they named, like poured milk.

But I was forlorn and alone in the midst of my luggage when I was approached by a young sunburned woman with a child clasped in her arms. Then I noticed walking beside her a young man in a dark striped suit and white shirt which

he must have found uncomfortable in the already oppres-
sive heat of morning. He carried a tightly rolled umbrella.

Sue and Colin, of course! We exchanged the absurdities
which are commonplace when people meet after long ab-
sence; we marveled at Change, we had all changed, everything, everyone had changed. I experienced a sudden fear
when I remembered the game we had played as children,
setting our faces in a certain expression and waiting for the
wind to change, for when the wind changed our faces would
be set that way for ever, even in death.

Yes, we had changed, we lied to each other again and
again, with exaggerations of gladness. How pale Colin's
face seemed, as if in this climate of sun he had been denied
the very light which he had traveled so many miles from
his own country to experience and make his ally. Or was
the light in Spain as free as its abundance implied? Or had
Colin used so much of it for his painting that there was little
to spare for his body? And there was Sue, brown as that
gleaming kind of cough medicine where the light shows
through and which you know (and the advertisements say)
is filled with "goodness." Flourishing and maternal, she
clasped their little boy (Bobbie) in her arms.

We had lunch in a quiet square. Everyone was full of in-
quiries, excitements, dread, while little Bobbie, apart from us
all, chattered in fluent Catalan to the pigeons in the square.
As an explanation for Bobbie, Sue remarked mischievously,
"Remember that day on the beach, at Black Rock, when
Colin and I were buried in a grave of sand? Well, this is
Bobbie. Developed from Death, you might say."

We looked uneasily at one another. The first raptures of
meeting were concluded, and there seemed nothing more to
say. How could we fill in the few hours before my boat
sailed?

There was always food and drink. Colin sat silently sipping his wine. I felt embarrassed. I did not know how to speak to this stranger in the dark suit with his pale sad face. It seemed an impertinence to speak to him. It is no use trying to keep the past alive by recalling that though your skin changes every seven years, and your hair falls out and is replaced, you remain the same, the same. I could not believe that this was Colin. I did not see why I should believe that it was Colin. Yet no one had assured me that it was not he. One is always alone, there is no help, in deciding identity. I thought to mention painting. Was not Colin a painter?

"How is your painting?" I asked cruelly. "You still paint, I suppose?"

An expression of fear crossed his face, an eclipse of any light that he might have harbored for himself from this abundant southern treasury.

He did not answer. We did not talk any more about painting. They told me that they were returning to New Zealand soon. I left earlier than I had planned to catch my boat. They did not come with me to the wharf. They directed me, walking to the end of the street where we said Good-by.

"If ever I come back to New Zealand, I'll see you then," I said.

"Yes," Colin said. "We'll see you."

Then he added, smiling, "Good old New Zealand!"

"Yes," Sue said, also smiling. "Maybe we'll find our two graves in the sand."

They stopped smiling then, and Sue caught hold of Bobbie. They turned to go. Colin was looking about him in a puzzled way.

"See you," he said again, then he added once more, gazing up at the sky as if trying to judge the intended sentence of light, "Good old New Zealand!"

the triumph of poetry

When he was born they named him Alan, meaning that in future the area of himself would be known as Alan. The area of oneself is like a drop of ink absorbed by blotting paper, gradually spreading, blurring at the edges, receiving upon it other blots in different shapes and colors until finally the original is dim, indistinguishable, while the saturated sheet of humanity upon which it lies is cast as worthless into the wastebasket, and another sheet, a clean sheet provided by the advertisers, is placed upon the desk.

Alan was a bright boy at school. He was Junior, Intermediate, and Senior Chess Champion. He could play tennis and swim well. He was liked by his classmates. He enjoyed school.

"What do you want to be?" they asked him.

He was not sure. In the holidays when he was fourteen he

began to write verse, prospecting a trampled earth with a seam of gold shining through it. The gold was his cousin Lorna's hair, fluffed like wattle, rubbing gold dust on his fingers when he touched it, but only in his dreams. During the day he swam in an ice-cold mountain pool, with a knife between his teeth.

In his final year at school they repeated their question because they preferred to watch their pupils heading, like runners emerging into the sun, each to his separate lane with his number in bold letters printed on his body. They preferred the course to remain clear in order that, should they have occasion to cheer their pupils in times of darkness or dim light, they should not discover to their humiliation, when the course was again visible, that they had been giving encouragement to pupils running in strange lanes, wearing strange colors, or even to those who were refusing to run at all, those who lagged, content with musing on the scenery, even breaking away from their course, running cross-country where no tracks had ever been marked, and no flags were flying, and there was no one, no official, to greet them at the end!

"What do you want to be?" they asked him again.

He told them that he had decided to be a poet.

"That's not exactly a career," they said.

"We mean what do you want to spend your life doing? Teaching, medicine . . .?"

"I will get my degree," he said (he had won a scholarship to a university), "and then write poetry as my life's work."

"But how will you earn your living?" they asked him. "You can always be a poet as a side line, in your spare time—but how will you keep yourself?"

One needs to be kept, swept, turned inside out, shaken free of insects, polished, pleated, trimmed, preserved in brine which is collected in opaque green bottles from the sea or from tears which fall in the intervals between each death.

They said good-by to him at school. They smiled kindly as he went out into the sun.

"You go ahead, get your degree, perhaps take up teaching; then you might decide what you really want to do."

He did not cower in the sun's blaze. He turned and spoke angrily. There was also a note of puzzlement in his voice. Why did they not understand?

"But I already *know* what I want to do. I am going to be a poet!"

The First Assistant, standing at the door, walked a little way toward him; there was a smell about him as if he had emerged from a stable where he had been fed on chalk; his gown lay like a bridle over his shoulders, and his eyes were trained not to stare distracted at the revelations in their corner mirrors.

"I used to write poems myself once, Wakefield. Who doesn't? I had a few published, in little magazines here and there. Of course I'm ashamed of them now. I had enough sense to leave that stage behind, get a safe job, regular income, marry, have a family, occupy my time in normal ways. I've seen boys like yourself go off to the University with bright ambitions. The important thing is to have something to fall back on.

The First Assistant glanced a moment at the door behind them, then he frowned; a gust of wind had banged the door shut. He stepped a few paces back toward the door, hitched his gown where it had fallen from his left shoulder.

"It's a phase, a phase, Alan," he said. He looked apprehensively behind him at the closed door. He seemed to be listening, as if his statement, "It's a phase, a phase," had assumed animal shape and was waiting inside to challenge him.

Then he opened the door and boldly walked in, out of the light.

Alan began his studies at the University. He wrote poems which were published and praised in the University Reviews and in a number of little magazines which kept bursting, pop, on the literary scene, and then folding, like delicate flowers, their petals leaning solicitously over their own broken hearts. It troubled Alan that there was so little time for writing. He wanted to write, of course he wanted to write, was he not bursting with ideas for poems, for stories and novels, yet where could he find the time between attending lectures, studying, flirting, making love, holidaying at the beach? Almost before he realized it, the University year had ended, and although he gained First Class Honors in his examinations, the amount of his literary work was very small.

"Why don't you take a job on the wharves in the holidays?" asked one of his friends. "I know someone who is writing a novel that way. He has chucked University and is working as a wharfie during the day and writing at night."

The proposal sounded interesting. Another friend told Alan of a poet who was working as a postman and writing in his spare time. In fact, the friend said, it was the fashion for poets to work as postmen; indeed, housewives were beginning to look suspiciously at the uniformed civil servants who flung their letters through the regulation letter boxes; for poets were questionable characters whom you could not see working, as you could see other people, in whirling activity like washing in a washing machine.

Poets no longer brushed the passion from their souls like dust from a plum, by writing about kowhai trees and the felling of the bush; no, they retired to their own houses, pulled down the blinds, disconnected the telephone, cut off the electricity, and in the darkness and isolation they were sitting down like Little Jack Horner to try to crack the stone of the plum, and everybody knew that fruit stones contained arsenic which was of course a safeguard against the self-congratulatory phrases of Little Jack Horner, What a Good Boy Am I. . . . But the secretive way of writing was inclined (Alan's friend told him) to rouse envy in people, to make them wish that they too could work in secret instead of being exposed like washing in a washing machine; and this (Alan's friend told him) made them inclined to sabotage washing machines—and poets!

"I'm a novelist myself," Alan's friend said. "But a poet working as a postman is a risk, and housewives know it. Can poets be trusted to carry and deliver private communications? Ever, even in their own writings?"

And Alan's friend pointed out the dangers to poets and to the public (multiple dangers if the identity of the two coincided) of sorting mail in small caged rooms; of franking with strange marks invitations accepted or rejected, summonses to appear in court, eviction orders, declarations of love and hate, notifications of death, and the dead letters themselves, address not known, addressee departed leaving no trace, deceased. . . .

For the holidays, then, Alan did not work as a postman. He found a job as porter in a hospital morgue, attaching tickets and tying toes together, and looking for vacant spaces on the shelves of the refrigerator in order to keep a state of efficiency. He found that the atmosphere stimulated his thinking, but only while he was among the corpses, for as soon as he went to his digs to carry out his plan of writing at night, his thoughts seemed to vanish. It's the revenge of the dead, he complained, being at that time inclined to generalizations and simplifications, chiefly because he was tired and felt in need of a milestone to rest against, or if not a milestone as they were now historical treasures and no longer legitimate resting-places, a road signal, ROAD UP, DANGEROUS CORNER.

But he knew it was not the revenge of the dead. Their toes were tied with pink tape, in bows, as for a festive occasion. Their faces were in unsealed envelopes, forwarded at half-rates with five conventional words of greeting. All was in order. The dead did not need revenge.

Before the beginning of the next University year Alan found it hard to decide between continuing his studies and finding a job as a wharfie, farm roustabout, shearing hand, freezing-work hand, sharemilker, milk-bar attendant, or waiter in a tourist hotel. Or postman. Then he met Sylvia and instead of being afflicted with the recklessness of a lover, climbing hazardous mountains, plunging into milling torrents, he put on his oldest clothes and sat all night on the beach, threading and tightening possibilities, like a poor fisherman mending a hole in his net.

He decided to be cautious, to continue his studies, for he realized that the net and the mended hole in it would be needed to keep out the rain when rain had the impertinence to fall upon Sylvia.

Do nets keep out the rain?

Alan decided Yes, after he had spent all night on the beach.

Such decisions are not taken lightly which does not prove that they are correct because their birth has caused inconvenience, only that they are defended with more passion than reason, as statesmen know, who carry tight-lipped umbrellas and receive blows to their pride.

Alan loved Sylvia. He courted her on the beaches and the

riverbanks and over the desk of the University Library where she worked. They married and rented a washhouse which they converted into a tiny flat. They had a folding bed, an electric cooker, two chairs, a table, a bookcase which held books instead of ornaments, and they shared a bathroom and lavatory with the young couple, Tony and Leila, living in the adjacent washhouse. Tony had been a stock hand in Australia and was now working on the wharves and writing short stories in his spare time.

"As soon as I see my way clear," he told Alan, "I'll be writing a novel. How's your poetry coming along?"

"If conditions are favorable . . ." Alan began. "We might be talking about prize flowers or a proposed truce in a long-drawn-out civil war. . . ."

"Perhaps a harvest of opportunities; reaped and bound, stacked by machine, but with no mechanical device for grinding; only two stones, gravestones. . . ."

Alan and Sylvia, Tony and Leila, were enjoying their married life although making love gave little time for study and less time for writing the poems and novels which it inspired. Then the long summer evenings were so pleasant! How lucky they were to be living so close to the beach where they could have picnic meals, dig down to Spain if they were so inclined, romp in the water, surfing, swimming, fishing from the rocks, or wandering hand in hand by starlight and moonlight, plodging their toes in the wet sand, their ankles entangled with seaweed, the stink of salt in their throats. Summer was wonderful and warm, no one could stay inside chewing at books, the sky in the daytime was pure blue, now solid, like rock so that you might have hammered it and been showered with lethal stones and pieces of blue cliff, now like bright blue glass that endured the sun until it shattered in a storm with lightning and thunder, and silver-wet outer space seeped through crackling like cello-phane, sheeting the hills with rain and mist.

Who could study and pore over novels in the summer?

Yet when the two young couples wandered along the beach in the evenings they liked to recite poems, but they were not poems which Alan had written.

"You have to get your voice right for mine," he said, laughing. "The salt air pickles my language, shrivels the skin of it; the roots lose their grip; my words are not endowed with prehensile characteristics."

They skimmed stones on the sea, stones cold as a turned-aside human cheek, if death can be defined as the lure of a new direction where eyes and face target the unseen.

They set crabs on one another, laughing when the pincers closed on the loved skin. They stamped and shouted; dived in the water and made floating love, merman to mermaid above the crusted wrecks of nothing and the discarded bicycle wheels and car bodies.

Life was idyllic.

At one time Sylvia discovered that she was pregnant. Her heart flurried with alarm. How could she rear a child in a washhouse? Besides, Alan was still studying, she would have to give up her job. . . .

Alan wanted her to have the child. He began (when he found time) to write poems about it, "Lines to my son, Aged Three"; "To My Daughter Lying in Her Pram"—

> My wild-west daughter in your covered wagon
> sombre
> waterproofed against the sky and the tears of
> your mother. . . .

One afternoon, however, Alan and Sylvia kept an appointment in a house in Freeman's Bay where both were blindfolded, and Sylvia underwent an operation. That evening Sylvia lay seriously ill in the local hospital, but after a few days she recovered, no questions were asked, and she and Alan resumed their idyllic life, less forty pounds of their savings, and with an unidentified fear which greeted them each evening in their tiny washhouse flat as if it were lord of their mansion. They chose not to identify their fear. Names, they realized, bestow space, keys, power on the nameless which encircle human lives, waiting their chance.

"How fortunate we are to be so intelligent," they said to each other when one night they came home to find their fear standing waiting for the double bed to be unfolded for love and sleep.

Soon it was Alan's fourth year at the University. He had gained a brilliant degree and was sitting his Honors Examination. He found little time for writing poetry.

Leila and Tony had sailed overseas where Tony was to seek his fortune and where he would find time for writing his novel.

There was a prevalent idea that Time overseas was different from Time in one's own country; it could be juggled, coaxed, extended in a most extraordinary and satisfying manner. Leila and Tony were already installed in a tiny flat in London and their first letter (they had written no more since their arrival) had been enthusiastic and full of plans for the future. It did seem, Alan thought wistfully, that Time overseas was more abundant, looped and lazy like spaghetti, dangling everywhere, one only needed to twirl a fork of thought and hook an endless length of Time.

Occasionally, however, Alan would set to work and produce a poem which he sent to one of the literary magazines. He was beginning to gain a reputation. One or two people spoke of him as "that promising young poet Alan Wakefield." Another had remarked, in rather sinister fashion, Alan thought, "Alan Wakefield is a poet who should be watched"; while yet another critic noted that it was "impossible to judge Alan Wakefield until he has given us a small but representative volume of his work."

I wonder, Alan thought, reading the critics' words, if I have enough poems to make a book, to submit to a publisher? Oh, if only I had more time! What would I not do with more time!

How excited he became when he thought of the prospect of more time! It's like the old days, he would think, feeling a quickening in his blood and an acceleration of thoughts in his mind.

The old days, and he was only twenty-four!

Still, life was good, life was satisfying. He was studying hard for his examination. He was very much in love with his wife. He had many friends. There were parties, picnics, expeditions to the bush, to the mountains. People called at all hours to their tiny flat, "Hey Alan, anyone home? Hey Sylvie!"

Sometimes at night when all the visitors had gone and Sylvia, exhausted, had already fallen asleep, Alan would go to the tiny window of the washhouse flat, draw aside the skimpy lace curtain, and look down at the sea crouched moaning and restless at their back door. He would time his breathing to the sighing rise and fall of the water, and find himself sighing also, or moaning.

The patience of the sea depressed him. Why should it go on waiting and waiting, moaning and beating its forehead, shedding a fury of tears or, placid, swallowing them and shining with pretended peace, yet always waiting and waiting as if it were so sure of the outcome and the end?

Often Alan would watch the sea until far into the night.

166

Then he would start from his dream and think guiltily, I could have been writing a poem. Then he would try to console himself. "Still," he would say, "it's worth it to be able to observe all that beach in all tides and seasons."

"Worth what?" his muse and his conscience asked together.

Yes, he would think, I could have been writing a poem. He was beginning to think more often of writing poems than of the poems themselves. People talked to him of poetry. He began to feel hemmed in, as if people were trying to decide his life for him. "I don't have to write poems just because they ask me to," he would say. It seemed as if people were invading him, his private territory and putting up their own signposts. He resented this. There were times now when he stayed silent for days, and one or two of his acquaintances began to whisper amongst themselves and tap their foreheads, which was a means of charming themselves against their fate, or of waking up their thoughts which had overslept, or of trying to enter the perpetually closed mountain skull. Who knows?

Alan gained his Honors degree and was appointed to the post of lecturer at the University. Life was gay once more, social, controversial. Lectures took a long time to prepare. The weather that summer was again very warm. There were swimming parties to the beach, morning, noon, and night, moonlight bonfires and barbecues. In a quarterly review of literature one of the critics asked, "What has happened to our promising younger poets?"

That means Alan, of course, Sylvia thought as she read it, but she did not say so directly to Alan. Besides, he could no longer be called "one of our promising younger poets." His hair was thinning at the temples and a bald patch had appeared at the back of his head. It was early for Alan to be losing his hair, many kept theirs well into middle age or did not lose it at all, but Alan seemed to be subject to the pressures of a personal age which took its toll not by years but by a secret ringing, as of trees, of the life of his heart. The thinning of his hair was merely a concession to recognized Time, to allay the suspicions of those who, tiring of the marks of chronological age, might seek to explore the more secret areas of a man's life where Time is personal with its own rules and measurements.

The fact remains, Sylvia thought, that Alan can no longer be regarded as "one of our promising younger poets." Sylvia had an increasing desire to care for his poetry, to dress it to appear in public, to attend to the toileting of its language.

Also, a number of new poets were emerging from the schools and universities, and these were now appearing regularly in the literary magazines. Sometimes entire issues were devoted to "the new young poets." Once, when Alan was flipping through the pages of one of these magazines, he was touched to read a tribute to himself as "one of the country's established poets, Alan Wakefield, who pursues his own quiet line of thought."

Yes, Alan thought bitterly, a quiet line all right, a branch line about to be closed because nobody travels there any more and weeds are growing over the track; and everybody dizzies back and forth on the Main Trunk Line with stops for organized refreshment at fixed prices—yes, a branch line with no train and no timetable, no flags, no signals.

Yet the reference to his work inspired Alan to write a poem for the next issue of the magazine which was called *Trend III*, following upon *Trend I* and *Trend II* which had ceased through lack of financial support because poetry was not yet as popular as the T.A.B. and there was no legitimate reason why it should be unless it flashes winners and numbers in orderly and accurate gold lights that peck and stab like a surgeon's knife where one keeps one's heart wrapped snug against the fivers. . . .

Alan's poem, which was not printed by the magazine, began:

> For drowning in rock-pools the face-down-
> ward men
> find cupful of tide enough to evict from their
> human home
> the put-you-up and put-upon generations of
> breath. . . .

His poem was confused and chaotic. It dealt with the stifling effects of teacups, teaspoons, phials, eggcups, eye-baths. . . .

Then came verses which Alan would have been ashamed of writing five or six years before.

> With the hairs of my head I trap
> the night-flying thoughts.
> My hair, like grass, covers the mountain
> where insects, knocking in the dark, are
> bruised upon the stone.
>
> Nude statues overgrown with glances,
> silent temples biding their time in the forenoon
> of civilisation,
> weapon-crammed outposts of the guiding
> touch,
> aphasic cities unable to extricate the knives
> and bullets of past utterance . . .
>
> Justice like an oilstove must burn
> with the correct blue flame

or the inhabitant of the room will die,
and the maker shed all responsibility. . . .

Green moss in the hollows between person to
    person calls,
drifts of snow; the telephone wires blown
    down;
beasts of prey encircling the stranded
    town . . .
Nothing has changed since I stood
in the Hangman's Wood.
Between thefts of death, night, and the arson
    of love
sounds the automatic alarm of light.
Still waits the noose on the hanging-tree,
still creeps the hooded assembly
of the declared honest brave and good,
still the sun carries its golden opinions and
    witnesses in the sky,
No, nothing has changed since I stood
in the Hangman's Wood.

Neptune, loyal to his nature, drives three
    white precepts home.
They are
Rest, Punctuality in meeting whirlpools and
    lagoons,
Patience in retaining more than a fair share of
    death.
These, say Neptune, are the trident of success
to sustain, to lean upon,
to thrust in three places through the hearts
    of enemies.
But *I* say, only jocularity and age

would burden *my* loneliness with three white
  precepts.
Salt grinds in the great wound everywhere,
more than two-thirds the surface of life.

Alan's poem rambled on thus. When it was returned to
him he tore it to pieces and flushed it down the lavatory. He
rarely wrote another poem, but now from time to time he
reviewed books of poetry, and his reviews were printed in
the back pages of the small literary magazines.

"Mr. Walters," he wrote in one review, "has twenty-two
wombs, seven bloods, eight, six, nine, fires, ices, bones, re-
spectively, three thighs, one cornucopia. Mr. Walters is indeed a composite wonder with immense physical, geological,
decorative, but few poetic possibilities."

The reply came from Mr. Walters in "Letters to the
Editor."

"There is nothing left but sour grapes to quench the dry
mouths of a certain academic coterie."

Mr. Walters (Ted) was a promising young student who
had abandoned his university career for poetry and who
earned his living working as a shearing hand, a rabbiter,
sharemilker, and, at Christmas, a postman, furthering the
exchange of robin-stained holly-festooned blood-robed plat-
itudes.

Two, three, four years passed. Alan was now a Ph. D.
Sylvia still worked in the University library. With an in-
crease in Alan's salary they bought an old colonial house in
the fashionable suburb of Tuapere. They had enough money
now to buy books, records, to attend concerts and plays, to
give parties. Although Alan worked hard preparing his lectures, and although they were witty, insightful, his manner

of delivery had grown increasingly hesitant. Where he had once been noted for his forthright delivery, his clarity of speech, now he was often inaudible; he had picked up irritating gestures, such as waving his hand vigorously before his face as if he were trying to remove not a massive obstacle but a congregation of small ones which clustered in more formidable solidity, threatening his line of perspective; sometimes he would draw his head briskly back as if in bending it forward he had thrust his face into invisible prongs. He would gaze toward the far wall of the old-fashioned tiered lecture room, at the students sitting in the distance, close to the roof, staring down at him like planets. A feeling of irritation and dismay would come over him as he wondered what exactly they were writing in their lecture books, and what they scribbled on the notes which they passed endlessly to and fro during the lecture. Perhaps one of them had ideas of being a poet? Perhaps he was writing poetry? If this thought occurred, Alan would be seized with a sense of responsibility, as if it were his duty to perform a particular act, to give a certain piece of advice, but always the urgency faded and he was left standing there, slightly dazed, with his notes propped on his lectern and the students waiting, some politely, others restlessly, for him to conclude his lesson. In appearance he seemed now far more than thirty. He was stooped. He was almost bald. The blue veins of his head intertwined like lines on a map of the world.

Sylvia had grown more beautiful over the past years. She was plump and matronly. She had the appearance of being a mother though she had borne no children, a fact which was outwardly accepted and faced by herself and Alan, but which was the cause of friction with relatives, for their respective parents grew more impatient as year by year they failed to achieve the status of grandparents (both Alan and Sylvia had been their only children). There were from both the Wakefields and the Simpsons, visits, whispers, suggestions, remedies, hints; clothes were knitted, toys were bought; even lists of names were drawn up.

"We are happy, aren't we?" Sylvia said to Alan. "We have almost everything. And we love each other."

Yes, they loved each other, and every night when they went to bed, the fear which they were intelligent enough not to endow with a name and power, crept between the sheets with them and lay next to each of them, warming itself at their skin and picking at the leftovers of their day's thoughts, lifting the flaps of their dreams to read their secret desires, trying with all its tiny power to find an identity.

But Alan and Sylvia were wise. Don't you think they were wise?

How happy they were!

"Fancy," Alan said, "Can you imagine that I wanted to be a poet?"

Suddenly he yearned for Sylvia to say quickly and fiercely, "Yes, Yes." But she laughed and looked at him fondly and said, "No, I'm afraid not."

They were very devoted.

She kept the home neat and employed a gardener to attend to the shrubs, for their section was nearly two acres, while she often worked in the garden with the flowers. She bought packets of seed and planted them in borders, and was so disappointed if the blooms did not match the illustrations in the catalogue.

"I should learn from experience, shouldn't I?" she said to Alan one day when one of the dahlia blooms was attacked by disease and died.

He smiled affectionately at her. He knew that she was

particularly clever with dahlias. He was sitting in the corner by the bookshelf, opening the packet containing the latest edition of *Seascape*, the literary quarterly, and wishing that the dispatch department had not made such a complicated parcel with so much useless string. There were none of his poems in this edition. He rarely wrote poems now. Sometimes, in a panic, in the night when Sylvia was asleep and the house was quiet, he tried to discover his excuse for not writing any more. It was not lack of time; it had long ago ceased to be lack of time. What was the excuse now? He tried desperately to find it. Age? Glands? Contentment? But who was contented?

He would have been happier if he had written a book of poems—just one book, a slim volume between hard covers—with the title on the outside and the dedication on the appropriate page. "To Sylvia, my wife." Or "To Sylvia."

He loved Sylvia more than ever. He loved the way her body had acquired a plump stored look, like a well-filled larder. He had the feeling that in some way she would provide for him. He was alarmed one evening when he was considering his dream of a book of poems with a dedication to her, "To Sylvia, my wife," and he found himself murmuring instead, "For self-service stores everywhere, for the brave, for the watered-down dreamer, for dried-up ponds full of dead frogs, caked with mud. . . ."

No, no. For Sylvia. Her dahlias are more wonderful this year than ever before; she has green fingers in the garden; she has been born to it.

Then from his seat in the corner by the bookshelf he had smiled fondly at her. He told himself how intelligent she was. Two intelligent people. They kept up with the trends in modern art and literature. When the National Orchestra played at the city festival each year they always bought tickets. They visited the Art Galleries. He subscribed to overseas journals, to poetry magazines from America, to one in particular called *The Triumph of Poetry* where in his student days he had been given a commendation in an annual award. "Just imagine. Alan Wakefield, a commendation in America," people had said. Now, each year when the award was made Alan would eagerly turn the pages of *The Triumph of Poetry* (Has my *Triumph of Poetry* arrived? he would ask Sylvia as soon as he came home on the twenty-fifth of each month) and study the winning and commended poems and compare them with his own of so long ago. How absurd, he would think. But people in literary circles still spoke of his poem. It had gained him a kind of national distinction. After all, America . . .

He sometimes felt ludicrous when he had been asked to take part in a radio book panel and the chairman's introduction referred to him as "the poet who was commended in *The Triumph of Poetry* award for promising young poets," while the other members of the panel, waiting impatiently for their own credits, would gaze incredulously at his thinning stooped figure and his bald head. Alan was a valued member of the book panel. He was an astute critic. His wit was sharp. Only his voice lacked the sense of urgency which made it compelling to listen to in the days when he had not enough time to write. He talked ramblingly as if all urgency had lost itself within him, or as if in traveling from him it had suddenly disappeared, like something wading out of its depths in unknown seas.

Alan Wakefield. One of the trees of lost poets who contribute to the shade, magnificence, density of the forest, who give concealment, food and space to tiny hibernating metaphors, the parasitic clichés, the feathered notions, the furred images that are so often slain and their coats transformed into collars to protect the necks of human beings from strangulation, and into muffs to warm in the winter season the pickpocket pickheart fingers.

A lost poet. A man with a little talent and not enough time; the promising poet who never fulfilled his promise; thwarted by sociology, circumstance, self.

But is not his life happy? He has a loving wife, a home, a secure job, an academic reputation. He interests himself in current affairs, oppressed peoples, decimal coinage, imports and exports, swimming (they own a beach house in the subtropical north where they spend every Christmas); and he is passionately devoted to literature, painting, music, the theater. He and his wife know how to cook continental food. . . . Some day they will travel overseas, perhaps visit Tony and Leila who have a luxury flat in Kensington, since Tony saw his opportunity and joined a literary agency of which he is now a director, marketing the works of scores of well-known and flourishing authors. . . . Tony and Leila go for holidays on the Continent; once they visited the United States. . . .

Yes, Alan is surely happy! He and his wife are intelligent, they enjoy good conversation, they have interesting tolerant friends who prefer to send ideas rather than people to the scaffold for murder, to lash intolerance and bigotry rather than the flesh of human beings. Every day brings so much to do, so much to discuss, plans to be made, letters to write, invitations to answer, lectures to prepare. And for Sylvia there is always the garden. How enthusiastically she prepares for each season!

It was late summer, merging into autumn with the lack of drama which disappointed Sylvia when in her gardening diary she checked the outlines of the seasons and their characteristic flowers. Summer each year took up so much room, leaving so little time for autumn. But summer was wonderful, so carefree and warm, and you walked with next-to-nothing on when you went shopping, and you swam day and night in the warm Pacific or, across the other side of the island, in the Tasman surf, riding in on the crests of the waves, picnicking by moonlight, wandering here and there, restless, turbulent as the sea. . . .

It was late summer.

Alan was on his way home from the University. He had not taken his car, and was traveling by tram. It was the last tram running in the city, the others having been replaced by trolley-buses. Alan enjoyed riding in the tram, sitting on the worn brown seats barred like washing-boards, rocking back and forth along the rails, strap-hanging when he got up to give his seat to a woman and her two children. It had been so long since he had traveled this way; it was so much easier to take the car. A feeling of exhilaration surged through him as he alighted at the stop and watched the tram rollicking by, noisy, exuberant.

"And it's not even spring," Alan said to himself, trying to explain his joy as he turned the corner into the quiet street where he lived. But as he walked by the gate and into the garden of his home he was surprised to notice the beauty of the flowers; he had not realized, he thought, what patience and time Sylvia was putting into the garden. The dahlias lined the path, right up to the house. There was one dahlia which was particularly beautiful, hacked with fire, its ragged petals chopped with fire, lined with red silk, overskirt upon overskirt of burning silk; alone it would abolish night.

He picked the dahlia.

"I'll write a poem," he thought, excitement surging through him.

"I'll write a poem. 'To my wife Sylvia upon plucking the first dahlia.' "

He hurried up to the house. Sylvia was out. He remembered that she had a meeting—a meeting where? He did not know, could not remember. He noticed when he changed from his dark suit that she must have been wearing her new dress, the one she bought for the Silverstone's party.

He did not stop to find anything to eat but went quickly to the room which he used as a study, and placing the dahlia upon the desk in front of him, he took a sheet of paper and wrote

"To my wife Sylvia upon plucking the first dahlia."

What a pity, he thought, that the seasons are not dramatic in the north, that first flowers do not burst upon us with shock. How she must have cared for them, he thought, stroking the petals which drooped a little and had stains on their tips, like inward bruises.

"To My Wife Sylvia upon plucking the first dahlia."

"True to tradition," he said. "A dedication at last. And we used to sleep like two mice in a matchbox, in a bed that dropped obligingly from the wall, in a washhouse fronting the sea!"

"A dedication," he repeated.

It did not seem to matter any more that he had not published his slim volume of verse. He was writing a poem to Sylvia.

He began to write.

> The quick brown fox noses the earth,
> the dog is lazy,
> and where are all the good men of the world
>   who will come to our aid?
> For now is the time, now is the time,
> while the quick brown fox noses the earth

Impatiently he scribbled over the nonsense he had written, drawing a face, a childhood face with deep eyes deep inside spectacles.

"To my wife Sylvia," he wrote once more.

THE PRISONER

In a dialogue with Time he said,
You handcuff me to humankind,
You sentence me who am the sentence.
When will you learn that I am nothing,
that giant mirrors are propped against your heart?
You sleep alone in your cell.
The twin delusional cell whose prisoner receives
    your sympathy and rage
is empty, thick with dust,
its lock eaten by worms and rust.

Alan considered what he had written. "It's poor," he said, "But if I start writing again something may come, I may yet write a complete book of poems. This is only a flexing of the muscles, so to speak. What is there now to hinder me from writing? Nothing, nothing at all."

His hand trembled. He could feel his heart pounding; he knew a slight anxiety in noting his heartbeats. Too much sedentary work? he questioned.

"But I swim. The sea is my second home."

Then Sylvia came in the door. She looked radiant. Yes, she was wearing the dress bought for the Silverstone's party.

"Writing?" she asked fondly. "Don't stay at it too long, darling." As a mother might talk to her child. "Playing trains, mud pies? Don't get your nice clean hands all dirty will you?"

Sylvia was quick to see that her approach had been wrong. "Take no notice," she said, giving him a quick kiss. "Go on writing as long as you like—it's the dinner that won't let you. It'll be ready in two shakes of a lamb's tail."

Then she glanced at the desk and noticed the dahlia, and a change came over her. Her voice was shrill.

"My dahlia!" she cried. "It's the prize one, the one I'm showing at the Society at the end of the week, I've been waiting and waiting for it to bloom. And you've picked it, you've picked it!"

She was almost in tears.

Alan was bewildered.

"I didn't realize," he began. He was staring at her in a dazed way. Out of all the flowers in the garden, did she recognize each one in this way? And the society, which society?

"Which society?" he asked. "What's the name of it, dear?"

"The name of the dahlia?" she said quickly. He could almost see her checking the list of names. How strange, she knew each one personally!

"The Dahlia Society, of course. Oh Alan!"

He stared. So she called them by names, she belonged to a society where they sat in a small room talking all evening about dahlias. . . .

"It's the loveliest one I've ever had, Alan! And you picked it. And look, you've bruised one of the petals! And is that ink on it, ink!"

Then she leaned forward suddenly and snatching the paper where he had been writing his verses she tore it to pieces. Then she seized the drooping dahlia and held it close to her breast. Then she began to cry.

"I'm sorry," she said. "Do forgive me, Alan!"

She picked up the pieces of paper and without looking at them she replaced them on his desk. He took a vase from the window sill and filling it with water from the tap in the adjacent bathroom, he tenderly took the dahlia from her and put it in the vase. He noticed a brown stain spreading in the water. Then he and Sylvia embraced. Everything was all right. They were intelligent, they understood each other. They went then to their dining room overlooking the garden. They had dinner, talking brightly to each other, making jokes. Alan told her about his journey home in the tram. How they laughed over it! How they yearned for the old days!

"Do you know," Sylvia said, "I passed our flat the other day, you know, the washhouse, and I couldn't resist knocking on the door. Do you know who lives there? You'll never guess!"

Of course he guessed, but he said "Who?"

"A young student and his wife, one of your students, too. He's going to be a novelist when he has time . . . I'm sorry. . . ."

"Don't pity *me*. You know that I was never much of a poet."

He hoped that she would say, "Yes you were, you were!" but she looked vague and sad and murmured, "Oh well!"

She brightened.

"Well anyway this young couple spend nearly all their time on the beach, the sea is so tempting, oh isn't it marvelous, quick as a wink the summer will be around and we'll be off up north; there's the garden though. . . ."

"You don't like leaving it do you?"

She was defensive.

"There's no harm in that is there? No harm in being fond of something. It was my best dahlia, Alan."

"I'm sorry, I've told you I'm sorry. I didn't know. . . ."

Her voice became sharp.

"You should have known. Oh Alan! We were so close! What has come over us?"

They went early to bed. He told her he had meant to write a poem to her, and she wept, and all was forgiven. They were very tender toward each other. They slept. Alan dreamed that writing a poem became so easy, all that was necessary was to take a packet of dahlia seed and spill it upon the paper. He took a packet of seed; it fell like fly-dirt, full-stops, pinpricks but Sylvia began to cry, it was her best seed, she said, the packet she had saved specially. Then she looked closer at the packet. She grinned. Her mouth was wide like a lake, and dark. No, she said, the best seed is at the Silver-stone's; this is the cheap variety which never blooms, I can't think how I came by it. She took the seed and tossed it out of the window and a huge bird flew down and swallowed it, stabbing his beak upon each grain.

"An indemnity," Alan said, and woke up. Sylvia was smiling in her sleep.

Soon the house was quiet. No one was awake, that is no one who had not his own right, like mice, traveling beetles, moths, beams of light; and the named fear who had at last been given power, space, keys, and lay supreme between Sylvia and Alan, waiting to devour their lives.